WHERE YOU ARE

TUCORA MONIQUE

B. Love Publications

Copyright 2019 © by Tucora Monique

ALL RIGHTS RESERVED.

Any unauthorized reprint or use of the material is prohibited. No part of this book may be reproduced or transmitted in any form or by any means, electronic or mechanical, including photocopying, recording, or by any information storage without express permission by the publisher.

This is an original work of fiction. Names, characters, places, and incidents are either products of the author's imagination or are used fictitiously, and any resemblance to actual persons, living, or dead is entirely coincidental.

Contains explicit language & adult themes suitable for ages 17+.

Synopsis

Kross Karmer is wedged between faith and fear.

After surviving a traumatic event that headlined her city's newspaper, the multi-talented beauty is unable to withstand large crowds and is paralyzed by the thought of history repeating itself. Shielding her mental stability and tucking away the will to rejoin the world, Kross becomes accustomed to her hermit lifestyle. However, with family, friends and a new delivery man vying for her affection; the eclectic music columnist has begun to wonder, is her lonely more peaceful than love?

Hollis Brown is seemingly satisfied with lust occupying the space for intimacy.

Years of twisted betrayal and deceitful partners have emptied the businessman's patience and faith in women. Outside of his daughter and Brown Brothas, nothing else matters. And yet, a lucrative wager amongst friends shifts the stern boss's focal and reintroduces second chances to a man who doesn't usually believe in re-dos.

Both canvassing between intuition and insecurities, will Kross and Hollis be able to find solace in the space between?

To my readers,
I write because words feel better when read.
Thank you for allowing me to make you feel.

To my children and my Geezy,
Thank you for teaching me how to feel.

CHAPTER One

KROSS

"Bend that ass over Rocky. I wanna see da sweetness you hidin' under that little ass skirt."

Obediently, I smiled. Giving the hungry hippo just enough of a lustful gesture to make his Vienna sausage stiffen like a hammer.

A groan that could have been mistaken for a moan snuck from my lips. I should have been familiar with his reaction; it had been the same every time he came to Body for his weekly feels. The same consistency went for my displeasure. I had to constantly remind myself that this experience wasn't about me. I had a job to do, and I was compensated for my discomfort. I wasn't the one shelling out fifteen-hundred dollars for feels and euphoria, so I had little to complain about.

Concentrating solely on my task, I gradually bent over in front of the wide businessman who sat on the end of the queen size bed gripping the navy-blue duvet. Like everything else in the establishment, the cover was overpriced and perfectly coordinated to compliment every piece in the room, including me.

Reaching out with sincerity, Porter tried to help; I slapped his hairy hand down. I didn't like for them to undress me. I wasn't a gift; my presence wasn't out of gratitude; it was all a part of the hustle.

Undoing the Nipsey blue sheer robe covering my stature, I exhaled once it dropped to the floor.

"You're so sexy. Worth every penny I pay to have you all to myself," he declared, his breaths transitioning into pants each time my hips completed a whine. The hoarse tenor of Jazmine Sullivan cruising through the room added a sultry vibe to what may have been mistaken for intimacy. Most women in this profession required drugs or alcohol to carry out the requested deed, I just needed music.

"Well, you know what they say. Exclusive ain't cheap," I replied jokingly, though I meant the statement wholeheartedly.

"Tuh, you can never be too much for me. I would give up everything in my world to keep seeing you. Our time together is fuckin' priceless, even if I've never felt the inside of you," he divulged as if it were something to be proud of. As if he didn't have a wife, he slipped up mentioning one time and probably kids he paid no attention too. There was no way, I should've been worth more than his world.

Gently, I pulled from his grasp and seductively turned my back, giving Porter a moment to enjoy the fruits of my labor in the gym. I didn't have a ridiculous ass, but it was enough to keep him distracted as I swallowed down paranoia that peeked after hearing his declaration of lust for me. There was no way in hell I'd call his sentiments love. What Roland and I shared was love, there was a huge difference.

Losing my thoughts in the lyrics of the song that shuffled on, I tuned Porter out until his threats became louder than the beat.

"Rocky, you're distracted. Let me call Kirk and see if I can get another little lady up here," he menaced. I knew it was idle. However, I entertained his statement with exactly what he was fishing for, desperation.

"Now, why would you do that?" I purred, my big lips pouting like a heathen trying to avert hell. There was no way he'd request someone else, but the sound of me begging him not to always made his dick stand as high as it could go. Getting down on my knees, I settled between Porter's parted legs and gently caressed the bulge serving as an interlude between us.

"I am so sorry for not giving you all my attention. What can I do to make you keep this between the two of us?" I quizzed, staring up at him.

Per usual, his yellow skin flooded with red and his breathing accelerated. "Rocky, I don't know…"

"Please? Just let me make it right and this could be our little secret. We've shared plenty of secrets over the past nine months, right?" I baited, sitting back on my feet and slowly removing the spaghetti straps of my Fenty negligee.

Nodding, firm on not breaking eye contact, Porter played along with the tug of war and shrugged his shoulders at my proposal. Biting my bottom lip, I waited for him to direct me as if I was none the wiser regarding where my invitation would lead us. He'd stroke himself to an orgasm and release wherever his conscious advised. Aside from the reputation of Body, there were girls, like me who decided to draw the line above our waist.

"I guess I can let you taste it a little. You know, how I like it," he ordered, pulling my head down dramatically.

"Make it nice and wet how I like it, or I may have to report you," he concluded, going on with the charades, as I prepared to get down to business. My mouth hadn't wrapped around Porter's piece before we both froze at the statement booming throughout the halls of Body brothel.

"You broads are going to pay today," I heard a voice repeat for the second time harshly.

"Who the fuck is that?" Porter spat rhetorically, pulling his pants up and his tank top down. My arched brows furrowed in confusion until the sound of gunshots altered my temperament into straight fear. Porter's mug matched mine, his strides to the door came to a halt.

Pow! Pow!

"What the hell is happening?" I murmured repeatedly, wondering where the hell security was. I didn't need an answer to know something bad was carrying on, on the other side of the door we waited behind. Loud screams and gut-wrenching pleas were muffled but heard. My body shivered hearing the gunfire pause then ensue. The sounds were substantial like mini bombs were dropping, intruding on happy endings vacant of intimacy.

"Rocky, Rocky!" Porter's hands were gripping my shoulders; shoulders he had just been nibbling on for sport minutes ago. Crazy, how life can change in a split second.

Jolting my body like a weightless doll, Porter motioned towards the corner bathroom while I stared at him with terror snatching the hydration from my limbs. I couldn't listen to his distress and pay homage to the footsteps that resembled drums marching down the third floor of my parents' brothel. My balanced tears leaped at the smell of gasoline, and the voice filled with hate that sounded like it belonged to a woman.

Shaking my head, I couldn't think clearly. "What the hell is going on?"

"Let's go!" The desperate man pleaded, his hand starting to shake the louder the person outside the door spoke.

"Porter," she sang menacingly. "I know you're in there with your little whore."

"Jackie?"

"You know that crazy bitch?" I screamed, regretting the day I didn't follow my brother out the door and away from this place.

Bursting through the only barrier we had, a deranged woman dressed in leather from head to toe with a purge mask shielding half of her face, entered waving a shotgun between the both of us. If my bladder was full, it would've been on the floor. A floor, I could no longer feel beneath me. My optimism seeped away with every tear that fell.

"Tell her who I am, Porter. Tell her I'm your wife of twelve-years and after all this time, you still can't stop hurting me by satisfying your fucking self." Without warning, the crazy broad smacked me upside the head with the barrel of her gun. It hurt so bad, I couldn't express it verbally. Even when she poured liquid on the floor I rested on, I didn't mumble.

Blubbing like a distraught victim, Porter dropped to his knees, ironically, exactly where I was just positioned.

"Jackie, I'm so sorry. I know I fucked up, but this? What have you done?" he cried while a new person, dressed the same, joined the side of Porter's wife. "We gotta go. Now," she demanded.

"You brought your crazy ass sisters with you? You crazy bitches are about to spend the rest of your lives in the pen. I couldn't have been worth all of this?" he shrieked. I still hadn't mumbled another word. All I could think about was how I wasn't supposed to be here in the first place, and how this was all my fault. How Porter was a client I snuck in for my own selfish reasons, and now we were about to die.

"You got one thing right, Porter. You weren't shit," the armed woman decided, sending a clean shot in the center of my highest paying customer's head. Blood splattered onto anything within a few feet of him.

"Oh my God. Oh my...please, don't," I started to beseech as she turned her hammer on me.

Grinning, she exhaled deeply. "You know what? I'm not going to kill you. Since you love being with my husband so much, I'm going to leave you in this little room to burn with him. Then you'll know exactly what it feels like to hurt so much, you'd rather die," she claimed, as I did my best at covering my face and vital parts once she threw a match on the fluid littering the floor. She'd already hit me with the butt of the gun, I couldn't afford another blow like that.

It seemed like I sat there for ages, I couldn't take my eyes off Porter's body. My body wouldn't allow me to move, but my brain couldn't take the notion of burning alive. In a daze, I drug myself to the bathroom we'd been attempting to get to. My air supply shrunk as I crossed the door's threshold. Coughing like I was in a cake session with Snoop Dogg himself, I passed out from the smoke snatching my ability to inhale and prayed my good intent was enough to get me into heaven.

"Tell me what's on your mind?"

"That was the first time I've told that story and not broke completely down," I shared, modest at my own growth. I was finishing up a session with my therapist, and usually by this time, I was drowning in either my tears or guilt. Today, I felt neither.

"That means your development hasn't been in vain, though you're still isolating yourself."

"Here we go," I grumbled, knowing where her statement was headed.

"Oh, yes ma'am. Here we go. You will never be able to fully reclaim your independence or your life until you get out that house," she counseled, pulling her glasses to rest on the bridge of her pointed nose. We both knew they weren't prescription, faking ass.

"I'm here with you *now*," I replied, smiling brazenly.

"For the first time in eleven months!" she pointed out. I remained quiet because she was right. I hadn't been physically present for a therapy session in forever.

"Though I'm extremely proud, it's time we start working on transitioning out of this hermit nature you've boxed yourself into. You're twenty-eight and spending your days hiding in your home."

Nodding, I plucked the strings of my imaginary guitar for comfort as I often did.

"Look, don't misunderstand my request. Seven people were killed, and many others including you were injured that night. You lived through that, and I want you to take advantage of the privilege. No matter the reason for her action, Jackie Porter's dealings were outrageous and so is how you're living situation. Get up and get out, Kross. You were given a second chance for a reason."

CHAPTER Two

Hollis

"Where the hell is Nico?" I spat, marching into the employee lounge of Brown Brothas delivery services like the feds raiding a trap house. For the third time today, I received a grievance that a specific driver was late with a customer's package. That shit was unacceptable. With companies like UPS and Fed-Ex serving as my competition, I couldn't allow customer service to be the reason I lost money.

"This isn't your living room foo', put your damn feet down," I barked, already knocking Rock's big ass boulders down off the wooden table.

"Man, don't chew us out because a fein is doing exactly what a fein does. Told you not to hire that bum in the first place and now you see why," Rock reacted, speaking words I'd already reminded myself of. I only put Nico on because he's family and he needed to be employed to stay out of jail. His ass was nothing like his older brother Rock, who only worked for me to earn extra money while in school. I started my delivery company five years ago and promised I'd help folks from my world when nobody else was willing to give them a shot, but Nico was taking advantage of my kindness. He, himself knew that was a fucking mistake.

"And let's not forget you fucking Henry's wife, resulted in that nigga quitting too. Talk about short staffed," one of my employees' voiced.

"Mind your business. Just like I told that nigga, I didn't know Shelby was his wife."

Laughing, Moses commented in a low whisper. "Like that would've made a difference."

Ignoring him, I snatched the refrigerator door open, and pulled out an empty water jug.

"What the hell is this? You niggas are horrible! This isn't your fucking house," I bellowed, slamming the steel door. Sighting my hands shaking, I balled them into fists, shut my eyes and exhaled deeply. None of the men in the room spoke or interrupted my moment. Once I quietened myself, I opened my eyes to a smiling Rock. Since we were kids, I had a screwed-up temper. One that should've belonged to a grown-ass man, but since there wasn't one present in my household there was room for mine.

"You straight?" my cousin asked, concern at the helm of his tone. Rock was a big dude, and his endearment for people matched his stature. Though that was hardly evident when his brother Nico, was the topic of discussion.

"Aye, boss man. I don't know if this helps, but I saw Nico's bike over on Figueroa and Lennox last night on my way home."

"And you didn't think to call me?" Rock interrupted.

Smoothing back gelled hair, Moses scoffed. "What I look like making a call on a grown man? That's not my business."

Laughing, Joshua, the newest dude on my team added his two cents. "But you just told where he was a second ago. What difference would it have made?"

"Aye cut all the arguing. Nico is out, I don't have time for this shit. I'll take over his deliveries for a few weeks. If anyone else wants the hours, they can pick up a shift until I find a replacement. I'll ask the dudes who work nights if they want in too," I ordered getting ready to leave.

"You can have that route all to yourself, bruh. Don't nobody have time to deal with the lady on Peach Street. Her big ass dog is hardly chained up when it's out, and she's always barking from that damn intercom," Rock complained.

Nodding, Moses agreed. "The last time I went over there she'd just got that damn Pitbull, and I made sure it was the last time I dropped off one of her packages too. Nico was willing to take the route, so we swapped."

"Oh, so that's why your scary ass flipped shifts," I teased, shaking my head at his reasoning. Dog or broad, there was nobody who could stand in the way of me getting my money.

"Call it what you want, but I bet you can't get her difficult ass to show face. I heard she was in a crazy fire, got a ridiculous payout and been in that house ever since," he shared, repeating the story like it was meant to scare me.

"Man, stop gossiping like a broad and get back to work," I demanded, waving him off. Moses had been on my payroll for two years and other than oversharing, he was a coo' dude.

"Yeah, I know, wave me off. But I bet you can't get Ms. Peach Street to open up. I highly doubt she's anything like those cheating hoes you entertain. Shelby and her husband both going crazy looking for you," he joked, knowing he was doing too much talking.

"I'll bet you a rack you can't get her crazy ass to step outside," the gambling man continued.

Looking over my shoulder, I glared at my cousin. Rock had always played on my good nature when I was about to get myself into something fucked up. At thirty-one, I still trusted him with my conscious. When I saw Rock shrug, I walked over and extended my hand to a hyper Moses.

"Don't worry about who the hell I entertain, ain't yo business. And no woman is that hard to crack unless you don't have the power. Remember, I know where you live and work when it's time to run me my money," I summed up with a crafty grin and an easy rack already in my pocket.

An hour later, I was standing on the porch of one of my biggest spending customers who didn't have any quarrels about what he loved most. When I saw him power walking towards the door, I frowned.

"Aww, come on Mr. Copper, put some clothes on! I don't have time for the speech about you and your balls today, man," I complained.

"You always gripe, but you can really learn something. A nudist lifestyle is a free lifestyle. Bet if I was a big booty woman standing here, you wouldn't have your face scrunched up," he had the nerve say, his dark skin in serious need of some damn oil.

Covering my eyes with one hand, I handed the old head his slip to sign with the other.

"Uncover your eyes, boy. It won't change the facts," he blurted, attempting to pull my hand down.

"Trust me, Mr. Copper, if a seventy-year-old woman with a stomach sitting on her thighs and hair everywhere answered the door as you do, I'd react the same way. No bias here, sir," I insisted, stepping back.

"You so damn immature," he barked, snatching the package from my grasp and slamming his front door in my face.

Gripping a handful of my twisted uptown fade, I growled bolting back to my truck. Times like these I had to remind myself why I put up with inconsiderate employees and entitled customers. I didn't have a rich uncle somewhere that I was waiting to die, I had to work. The least I could do for myself was make sure my hustle was on my terms and not to lace someone else's pockets.

Checking my route sheet, I cursed spotting "Ms. Peach Street" as my next drop off. I had dealt with enough bullshit for the day, but realizing she was my last stop eased the brewing tension inching over my endurance. I didn't give a damn about what this lady had been through, we'd all gone through shit so she'd have to find somewhere else to place the misguided aggression.

Twenty minutes later, I was jogging up the few steps leading up to a modern constructed home. There was no Pit in sight and thankfully, the rain was minimal. Moving to press the silver intercom button near the doorknob, a raspy voice came barreling through, prompting me to jump back.

"Can I help you?" she asked.

Frowning at my own reaction, I spoke louder than necessary. "I'm from Brown Brothas, I believe this is for you." Motioning towards the box in my hands, I waited for her to open the door.

Quickly, the wooly voice questioned my presence. "Who are you?"

"I just told you. I'm here delivering a package from Brown—"

Rudely, the faceless woman cut me off. "I didn't ask where you are from, I asked who you are. I'm not illiterate, I can read the company name stitched on your jacket."

"Okkk," I hummed, unsure of how to respond initially. Having just endured one of Mr. Coppers' wild mornings, I wanted to avoid chaos.

"You aren't Nico, my usual guy."

"Really, I hadn't noticed," I mumbled. "I'm Hollis. Do you mind coming out to sign for this? You sound like you're over eighteen," I figured, hoping my forwardness would kill the increasing dispute.

"Leave it in the drop box."

I shook my head. "I can't. Delivery requires a signature."

"No, it doesn't."

"What the hell?" I grimaced, my eyes concentrating on the camera I knew she was watching me from.

"Look, lady, it's cold out here. I know you can see the drizzle coming down. I got other shit to do and you're being problematic. You coming out to get your package or not?"

"What happened to the days when the customer was always right?"

"You askin' the wrong person," I offered, shuffling my attention between my double-parked truck, and the direction of the complicated woman's voice.

"I really hope you aren't going to other peoples' homes with this attitude. I can smell your impatience through the freaking door."

"Yeah well, I smell a stench coming from under your door too, but I'm not gon' speak on that," I replied just to get under her skin.

"If the labels read *Vibez*, leave it in the box. Please."

Squatting, I noticed the area she was referring too.

"Wow don't tell me you aren't able to figure that out either," she refuted.

Scowling, I stood up straight. "Aye watch your mouth! You sayin' a lot behind an intercom and a heavy ass door. Must look like a mud duck," I declared, pulling the collar of my jacket up around my neck. I shivered, checking the time on my watch.

"Sir, your insults won't change my mind. Leave the damn package in the space allotted and walk away. And with a nose that wide, you shouldn't talk about someone being funny looking, Squidward."

The lightness that poured into her tenor pulled my attention back to the voice box as I turned to leave.

"I've already told you, the package requires a signature. I'm not compromising my business because you don't want to step outside without your wig on."

"I don't wear wigs, for your information. And if I did, I wouldn't be that superficial. Look, I'm telling you if the receipt requires a signature, it doesn't belong to me. I opt out of that option when placing orders to avoid *this* very thing from happening."

"You're weird," I growled, finally deciding to give up on persuading her to open the door. She could pick her shit up at the post office like everybody else.

On the last step of her porch, an extra insult chased me down the path.

"I'm weird, and you look like your breath stinks. Fucking knock off Iman Shumpert," she touted in the privacy of her home.

"But you wouldn't know what my breath smells like, weird-ass won't step outside to retrieve something you ordered. And trust me, that nigga wish he looked as good as me," I countered childishly, rushing back to her door as if I could get inside. After the day I'd had, my tolerance for bullshit was at a minimal and her speaking to me out the side of her face or some other part of her that I couldn't see, wasn't in her favor.

Pulling a piece of paper from my pocket, I let the scattered raindrops add moisture to its palate.

"Let's see if you'll bring your ass outside now," I mumbled shamelessly.

"What the hell are you doing? Don't do that!" She shrieked, though it was too late. I had already used the old receipt to cover the lens on one of her cameras.

I couldn't tell if her hysteria was real or some ploy to get me to back off but she should've considered that prior to running her trap.

"Asshole," the mysterious lady screeched.

"Bet you won't say it to my face," I clowned, hurrying to my delivery truck as the rain started to come down harder. I may have been dead wrong for blocking her vision to the outside, but she was wrong as hell for keeping us all at bay when I hadn't done a damn thing to her. Weird ass.

CHAPTER Three

Kross

"Kross, you know I love you, and I'm not discrediting your experience. I understand PTSD is real, but we miss you. You used to be so easy-going and optimistic, and now, things are so calculated. You can't spend the rest of your days in that house," Truth reasoned. I swear I was tired of people singing that same hymn, there wasn't much sincerity in the stake anymore. And sadly, the longer Truth stayed with my brother, the more she sounded like him. I could chop her sentiments up to hormones but that wouldn't have been fair to my nephew.

Making my irritation clear, I sighed into the receiver with force. "The advances of today's technology beg to differ. I don't miss a meal or a monumental event. I can order everything from steak to dick."

"Plastic dick!" My sister in law shouted.

"Not necessarily. Backpage may have gone out of business, but BBB has not," I countered, mentioning a male and female brothel that damn near put my parents out of business and who unlike our services, made house calls.

"Girl, please. That's nasty, and besides, you won't let a man into your house let alone your pussy."

Smacking my teeth, I didn't bother to respond to Truth's ridicule. She had been with my brother for too long, impatiently waiting on a ring until he learned to keep his penis in his pants. Now, don't get me wrong, Kennedy had turned over a new leaf in the last few years, but Truth's opinion of what I did or didn't do with my pearl didn't count.

"I don't mean any harm, Kross. I'm just being honest. You cannot say in confidence you don't miss the sensation of a man's touch, a real man. One who loves you beyond the pain that makes you unsure of his actions, even when he's showing you differently. The type of man that's okay with waiting on you to meet him in forever because he's confident you'll make it to where he is. How will you find him, Kross, if you remain tucked away?"

Truth's words lingered in the background when the sound of a large black truck stopping on my street, gathered my attention. Without fully thinking it through, my body ushered itself to my living room window.

"The fact that you believe healing includes a man invading my space is enough to conclude I shouldn't be taking advice from you," I contested in a low murmur. It was as if my eyes and lips couldn't move at the same time. The sight of Hollis lifting and shuffling boxes in knee-length shorts with the sleeves of his uniform shirt rolled above perfectly carved biceps, had my tongue hesitate.

Damn, he's fine, my conscious shouted without permission from my ego. Everything from his wide nose to his hickory complexion made me evaporate into pure water. I knew he was six feet six at the least and climbing him had somehow become a new goal of mine.

"You can fuss and deny all you want, but your ass better be at my baby shower at the top of the month. And before you make up some excuse as to why you aren't ready, let me remind you Dr. Sway already informed me and your brother that you two agreed that at the one-year mark of the incident you'd start being physically available," Truth proclaimed, pulling my eyes from their probing.

"What the hell happen to patient-doctor privilege?" I thought aloud, stress reverting to my disposition.

"That privilege went out the window when you decided to go to your big cousin for therapy," was Truth's quick rebuttal.

If Kerry Sway wasn't family, I'd report her ass to whoever needed to know about her running her big mouth. On the other hand, Truth was right. I'd made a promise to myself, my family and my doctor to rejoin civilization three-hundred and sixty-five days after the bitch who went mad was sentenced to life for her calculated crime; Regrettably, for me, that day was amongst us.

"Listen, I know how you are about public places now, so your brother and I ensured the guest list includes close friends and family only. Your parents probably won't show, and the location is close to your house. There'll also be no balloons and hardly any glass. If this is too much, you and I can start off by going to church together," she offered as if that was a safe resolution.

"Yeah, because a crazy person has never come shooting in a church," I chimed sarcastically.

Fed up with my mockery, Truth groaned. "Point taken, Kross. Just tell me you'll be there, and I'll leave you be."

"I'll think about it," I groused.

"You always say that, Kross."

"And I always think about it, Truth," I challenged, knowing she'd stay on the subject if I wasn't firm on my reply. Up until a few weeks ago, my sister-in-law supported my standards of living. She even convinced my brother to respect my process but obviously, Truth's feelings had changed. My time in the clouds was seemingly up and I was petrified to see what solid ground had in store for me.

NEARLY TWO WEEKS had passed and though I'd made the decision to support my family, I was scared shitless to actually go through with it. No matter how unconventional my childhood was, I would still consider myself spoiled. I never was forced to do anything I didn't want to and my parents were extremely open-minded. And now I was in a situation no one could bail me out of except for me. No matter how much Truth and Kennedy fawned over me and reiterate their love, I had to depend on myself. Roland disappearing when things got hectic was confirmation that I had to be okay withstanding good and bad days alone.

Exhaling a few times, I stepped from my truck and power walked to the entryway of the event space. I was grateful the rain was out of sight unlike last week when I went for a walk around my neighborhood for the first time in a year. Dr. Sway accompanied me and talked me through my protest and the abrupt car horns that caused my heart to fall into my ass. I felt like a weirdo losing my mind over simple things most people hardly pay attention to. However, that was also what got me into the predicament I was in; I was oblivious to the things going on around me. I had become so content in my world, I stop listening to my intuition.

Once through the double doors, I smiled observing the Wakanda theme dressing white walls. Everything from the chairs to the appetizers was tailored to the cultural staple.

"Kross!" Truth cheered loud then swiftly adjusted her tone while pulling me in for a hug. I both hated and appreciated that she felt the need to censor her enthusiasm in my presence. It wasn't until recently I noticed the impact my emotional state was having on the people who loved me. My dad was growing wondered and my big brother was having his first kid for goodness sakes, yet I was acting like a baby my damn self. Other than my parents, I was all Kennedy had and it hurt to hear Truth say my brother felt I was leaving him hanging.

"I'm so happy you came. You look gorgeous by the way," the beautiful mommy to be complimented, a broad smile dressing her honey-colored face. My hair was freshly trimmed on the side, while the top was curly thanks to my latest house call; I wore little make-up and my outfit was simple. After hours of going back and forth, I decided on a pair of army fatigue cargo pants, a white button-down tied at my navel, and red vans to match my red crossbody. As always, I wore my Vibez bracelets and ruby studs.

"Your brother is going to be hyped when he sees you," she

beamed, dressed like she was photoshoot ready in a yellow gown that touched the floor and shined off her smooth coating. Rocking back and forth on the balls of my feet, my eyes shoot daggers around the room. I had no reason to be apprehensive in the company of my people but that didn't stop my fingers from endlessly stroking my guitar that no one else could see for relaxation.

Strolling over obnoxiously, Kennedy rubbed his hands together greedily. A small grin captured his handsome face as he neared us. I was grateful to see his smile. Kennedy wasn't the nicest person and after the disaster hit our world, he was worse.

My big brother wanted to bash the skull in of the woman responsible for allowing her bitterness to become bigger than her conscious. However, once he became content with the notion that that was impossible, the natural protector was set on moving forward. I, on the other hand, couldn't let shit go *that* easily. I couldn't trust myself or the people I choose to know. Settling into solitary had felt safer than companionship. Not even the hefty check given to victims of the incident by her family was enough to shift my mental brawls.

"Look who finally decided to step out of hibernation," Kennedy joked, picking me up and spinning me around.

"Ugh, put me down foo'! I told you I was coming, so I'm here," I acknowledged. "Guess, it's time."

"You damn skippy, it's time! Shit, it's been time!"

Pushing away from him, I grimaced. "Says who? I could've sworn I'm the one walking around with second-degree burns on parts of my body."

"You also walking around with a quarter-million payout. Find the good in the grunt, baby girl," Kennedy declared with a red cup in his hand and too much of my business on his lips.

"Money isn't worth...everything," I debated, my voice lagging at the sight of someone familiar.

"Who is that?" I blurted. "I mean, how do you know *him*."

Glaring over his shoulder, my brother spotted who I was referring to.

"You talkin' about Hollis? That's my boss. He owns Brown Brothas. I told you I recently started a new delivery job."

"*You* know him?" Truth wanted to know. Her inquisitive expression was overflowing with humor and curiosity. Before I could either disappear or further interrogate, a man I had only seen in khaki's and polyester, infringed on our conversation.

"My nigga," my bother blurted, pulling Hollis in for a brotherly embrace. "I knew your ass would come. Talking about you don't do baby showers."

"Man, miss me. You knew when you invited me, I'd be here to support you," Hollis replied, his face too deep in his phone to notice me. Even so, when he did look up our eyes locked for the first time and everything around him became less significant. The subtle music playing in the background, light chatter of excited guest and even the shuffle of feet against the wooden floor were left in a haze.

"Who's this?" Hollis asked, his wide smile plastered and breaking my trance. His teeth were perfect, and the smooth facial hair covering his lower face worked. I mentioned it as an insult initially, but I thought it was a plus that he resembled Teyana Taylor's hubby. That man is built like a chocolate God and possesses the smile of a sly pimp. That may not be the best comparison, but hey, it's the best I got.

"Kross, this is my boss Hollis."

When the bold man, licked big enough to swallow mine, Kennedy jumped in.

"Aye stop staring at my sister like she's one of your broads," he shouted, ending the eye fucking both Hollis and I openly did. It took the restraint of a nun not to purr, just to get further under my brother's skin.

"Your sister, huh? I thought you said you were an only child," Hollis recalled. Before I could curse Kennedy out, the huge man spoke again. "I'm just fucking around. I'm Hollis. My bad if my staring offended you."

"Your joke wasn't funny, but I wasn't offended by the gawking."

When his even brows lowered, mine hiked.

"I know you from somewhere," Hollis answered taking a step closer to me. The smell of Gucci's *Guilty* stifled my verbal reply, so instead, I shook my head.

"That wasn't a question," he ordered, as he often did when speaking to me through my door.

"You don't know Kross from nowhere, so keep all that mack shit to a minimum. Boss or not, you'll have to see me from the shoulders over her," Kennedy acknowledged, slapping Hollis in the center of his chest. A chest this fool had the nerve to have on partial display with the first three buttons of his shirt undone. I tried to ignore that we were dressed almost identical, but it was hard as hell to miss.

"Check it, you know me, Kennedy. I wouldn't have said it if it weren't true," Hollis concluded, returning the aggressive chest action.

"I think you just got too much pussy clouding your mind, man. Let's go get you a drink," Kennedy suggested, pulling my delivery man from my visional grasp.

Retraining my focus, I asked Truth to show me to the table she'd reserved for me. It was in a dark corner of the room, and near an exit just like I preferred.

"Hey!"

"What?" I answered.

"Have something you want to share?" The pensive glare the waddling beauty gave was my warning to spill.

"You *do* know that man, don't you?"

Rolling my eyes, I couldn't contain the laugh that slid when recalling Hollis and I's anonymous arguments. Each time, he swore he was canceling my services, yet, the following week he'd be at my door giving me a hard time all over again. At this point, it had been almost two months. Divulging the little there was to tell, I groaned at Truth goofy expression.

"What?" I whined, giving a toothless grin to a few family members who walked by and waved shyly.

"That sounds like a wedding waiting to happen, sis. I don't know much about him other than he—"

"I didn't ask you about him, Truth," I recanted, shutting her down. "I know you're just trying to help but I have too many other things to rebuild right now, affairs of the heart are the last thing on my list of to-dos," I reasoned. And as if on cue, just as the declaration entered the atmosphere and settled on my common sense, my body grew anxious. The hairs on the back of my neck and those on my arms saluted the sky. When I recognized what caused my body to panic, my nipples pronounced themselves like every component of my senses.

Hollis was many feet away, yet my insides responded as if we were physically attached. He did nothing to disguise the hungry and familiarity he felt while watching me. I didn't know if it were my lack of physical attention or simple infatuation, but something had us tethered unbeknownst to anyone else in the room. I was supposed to be concerned with my surroundings, and here I was, again, allowing a man to sit in the center of my rationale.

Clearing her throat, my pestering love one stepped in. "Okay, I see you and I need to discuss this at a later time. I'll let you and Hollis continued to eye fuck each other in a room full of people, while I go make sure my auntie Gwendolyn isn't already making a to-go plate."

"Shut up. I'm not eye-fucking anyone, I'm watching everyone."

Standing, Truth fanned me off. "Girl, please. Try that with someone who doesn't know you. The same look you're giving that man is identical to your expression when opening fresh Swarovski crystals or writing for your column. Don't worry, we'll talk. In the meantime, I'll have Kerry bring your plate over," Truth explained, rushing over to my brother.

I smiled watching the tinman melt like putty in her hands. It took years for them to get it right, but once they did, nothing could compromise their union. Kennedy had worked in a brothel, been sent to prison, and got caught with his dick out on more than one occasion. For Truth he was worth the trouble and I'd never judge her for that, it wasn't my job to measure her patience.

The day was moving faster than I thought it would and my family turned out to be more casual than I'd given them credit. Most in attendance were my father's sisters, cousins and they're children. Ironically, they were all we had growing up after my daddy's profession manifested into property and my mom adapted to the notion of being his bottom bitch. Her family cut us all off, but let her tell it, my father was worth the suffice.

"I've let your behind sit over here long enough, come on out here and play a game or something. Ain't nobody gon' bite you girl," my daddy's oldest brother Smith, argued, pulling me from my seat before I could protest. Once on my feet, my hands snatched back at his consist touching and tugging.

"Let me go, Uncle Smith. I can walk," I blurted, much louder than intended.

"Girl lower your damn tone. Ain't nobody here gon' do nothing to you! Shootings happen every day and you want a party for surviving. Your parents taught you better than that," he spat, stilling my actions. Right as my mouth opened to remind him of some of the things my dad taught him, a reassuring authority covered my back.

"Is there a problem?" The person asked and I wasn't sure if he were speaking to me or Smith.

"Boy, this my niece here. She don't need no back up when talking to me."

"Shit looked different from where I was sitting. Family or not, the lady asked you to give her space. Back up, bruh," the deep voice bellowed over my head.

Trailing his large frame up and down, Smith grilled Hollis hard.

"Who the hell you supposed to be? Better back yo ass up before I have my son come over and see you from the shouldas, youngsta."

"That'll be his blood on his hands. Don't matter to me either way," Hollis concluded too calm for the subject matter. Noticing the stares starting to find us, I shut my eyes and calmed my anxiety. A second later, I was calming the situation.

"Okay look, we can't be the reason Kennedy and Truth's day is ruined. Uncle Smith, I appreciate you wanting to get me out of my shell, but I'm fine," I encouraged, pulling Hollis over to the game area set up in a corner of the room.

"You always take the flak for shit that isn't your fault? I saw how aggressive he was with you. You had the right to be upset," Hollis challenged.

"Some things aren't worth a fight. Especially, shit that's meaningless," I advised, trying my hardest not to keep staring up at him. When I saw Hollis position himself behind me, I recognized how the sentiment didn't make me uncomfortable.

"I was serious about what I said earlier. I know you from somewhere. Just like me, Kennedy grew up in this city, so I'm going to assume you did too." The strong-willed man refused to let his inkling vanish.

"Let it go, Hollis."

Concentrating, I listened to Truth explain the rules of the game we walked in on as about as five other couples prepared as well. Grabbing the utensils we'd need for the bottle-diaper contest, I handed Hollis the bottle. Frowning, the blunt man complained.

"Nah, I'm not feeling this. We can play something else," he recommended.

"Man up," I spat. "You act as if you've never sucked on—"

"You damn right. I'm not sucking shit! Never have!"

Playfully rolling my eyes, I took the bottle and handed Hollis the diaper that was seconds from being filled with mashed candy.

"Or you can eat—"

"Yeah, that sounds more like my speed," he interrupted, tapping my chin with his index finger. If I were a shade lighter, my blushing would've been on blast.

Taking our position, I waited on my cue to gulp down the bottle of apple juice. When the crowd's encouragement grew loud, I surprisingly found solace in my partner's eyes.

"You better be a pro. I don't take too well to losing," Hollis admitted, his long lashes fanning away any intrusions.

"And here I was thinking, it's just a game."

Laughing inwardly, Hollis shook his head. "It's never just a game. Never."

CHAPTER Four

HOLLIS

"Hi, Daddy! I thought granny was coming?" Connor asked opening the front door for me.

"Nah. I gotchu," I answered, checking her out for any hurt or harm. Other than the streaks of dry tears printed on her adolescent face, she seemed fine.

"Go get your shoes, and I'll be right out," I ordered, walking past my eight-year-old like my point of being here wasn't for her. I knew I could've merely come inside, got Connor like I told her grandmother I would and left, but I'd never been that simple of a man.

"Aye yo! Are you seriously in here gettin' busted down like a duck while your kid is in the other room?" I spat, busting in and filling Ciara's door frame as if I belonged there.

In the past two years, there hadn't been a time I came to check on my daughter and her mother wasn't doing something I felt was unacceptable. From having a houseful of bum broads over late at night, to simply not being home at all; Ciara wasn't taking care of Connor how she should have. I hated to admit it but my baby mama was a thirty-year-old, high school dropout who thought playing the government out of benefits was an accolade. I never acted like I was better than Ciara, just thought it was important to mention how much I'd outgrown her when she seemed to forget we weren't the same. Most times I steered clear of her, usually communicating with her mother when it came to our child. But even Ms. Jackson was fed up. She called me twenty minutes earlier explaining how Connor called her upset. From then on, I rearranged my morning and came to the other side of town to see about my baby.

"Ugh, what the hell are you doing here? I know my mama didn't *really* call you!" She had the nerve to yell, moving slow as a snail to unhook her body from the nigga she was bouncing on.

"Aye. Give us a minute, my nigga," I demanded, my jaws so tight I could feel my teeth gritting. Thankfully, ol' boy had an ounce of sense and disappeared behind Ciara's bathroom door.

Shielding her body with a worn robe, the ex from hell frowned deep. After years of a fast life and no brakes, the promising beauty went from resembling Kelly Rowland to something unfamiliar.

"He doesn't need to go anywhere. Get out of here with all the judgmental mess when you constantly have a different broad trotting behind you on the regular! Married ones at that! I have enough people on my back, I don't need you there too!"

Matching her tone, I invaded Ciara's personal space.

"Not with my daughter present to witness, I don't. You're teaching Connor the wrong way to move as a woman. And miss me with that childhood trauma. You've been putting that pain on a pedestal for long enough, stop reaching for it."

"And what the fuck do you think you're teaching Connor, always going back and forth between here, home and wherever else you run off to?"

"Man be real, I haven't touched you in over two years, so don't go there. I can tell you what I am teaching my princess, that a baby can't keep a nigga. You should be proving to her it's okay to be alone," I barked, causing her to flinch.

"You worry more about these fools and broads that don't mean you any good, than you do your own blood. You left Connor home alone last night and been locked in here with this bum since you got back. Your own daughter said that. It's cool, you don't want her; I'll take her," I ordered, going back into the living room where I was certain Connor was listening.

Close on my heels, Ciara shrieked. "You can't take her from me, Hollis! I'm sick of you taking shit from me, I have rights too!"

Ignoring her theatrics, I squatted low enough for Connor's eyes to align with mine.

"Baby girl, you want to come stay with me for a few weeks? Or do you want to stay with your mom? Be honest. I promise I won't spazz," I lied, knowing I'd have a fit once I got out of earshot. Connor was big on keeping the peace and would give any answer she thought would result in minimum strife. As a child, that shouldn't have been a concern of hers. When I heard Ciara clear her throat, I told Connor to listen to her heart. Peering over my shoulder, my eyes didn't need to meet the neglectful woman for her to grasp how thin my patience was. Ciara knew me and though I would never hit a woman, I'd end life in exchange for Connor's peace.

Palming my slightly hairy cheeks, the younger version of me grinned while pressing her forehead against mine.

"Daddy, I want to go with you, but only if you calm down. Anger usually results in accidents. My winter recital is in months, I have quite a few things to live for," she sassed.

"Exactly! Connor has school. Tomorrow is Monday, and we both know if she goes with you, she won't make it. She needs to be home, Hollis!"

"Why? So she can have you faking orgasms as a melody to fall asleep to? Get the fuck outta here," I confirmed, restraining myself from meshing her Rihanna sized forehead. "We rollin', babygirl?"

"Yes, daddy," Connor sang, snatching up her backpack from the floor.

"I love you, mommy," my sweet baby declared, wrapping her long arms around her mother's waist.

"When are you bringing her back, Hollis?" Ciara nagged above Connor's head.

I didn't give her an answer; I didn't think she deserved one. She and I didn't have a custody agreement, and oddly, she was more afraid of going in front of a judge than I was.

Pulling me out of the apartment, Connor and I remained quiet until we were in the truck and out the parking lot.

"Daddy. Do you hate mommy?"

"Nah. To hate, is to wish a person or thing is dead. I don't wish death on your mother, I just don't like that broad."

Shrugging, Connor fidgeted with her seatbelt strap. "I guess that's not the worst thing. I don't like corn and no one's losing sleep over that."

I thought to enlighten my baby on how I despising her loose mama and her disdain for corn weren't comparable but decided to leave it be. She was thankful for my answer and I was grateful for her contentment. And if you knew Connor, you knew content wasn't a favorite word of hers. She loved to challenge vague explanations and if she didn't tell you herself you wouldn't believe her age. Just like me, she was taller than most her age and her confidence was in check. More than once I reprimanded her for not keeping her appearance perfect. However, once she explained how trivial clean shoelaces were compared to her getting an A on her science project, I shut up about it. I'd tell her in a few years, it's possible to do both.

Truthfully, I begged Ciara to have an abortion when she said she was pregnant. When Connor was conceived, Ciara and I had been together off and on for two years. I had just gotten out of a complicated situation plus prison and she just didn't want to be alone. So much so that when I started working more hours to get the start-up money for my company, Ciara found solace elsewhere. We'd been apart for three months before she told me she was knocked up. I wasn't ready to be a father and I was honest about it. Ciara didn't give a shit about my concerns or apprehension; she was firm on her decision. It wasn't until I spotted her at a bus stop with my baby, a heavy ass stroller and pain covering her face that I recognized I wasn't being a man. My morals clicked on that day and I'd been ensuring my daughter never sat in the cold again for the last eight years.

Glancing at my passenger, I reached over and flicked her chin. "You coo' with working with me today?"

"Sure. If you pay me, I'm down," Connor negotiated sounding like her father, though she was her mother's twin. Just like Ciara, Connor had dark hazel eyes, thick brown hair, and a slender piglet nose and chin. The only thing she'd inherited from me was her height.

"How does a dub sound?"

"Perfect, if you're talking per hour. I'll even throw in box carrying and parking assistance," she grinned, her ponytail moving with every demand she laid out.

"How can I argue with such a convincing deal?" I inquired rhetorically.

"You can't. Just like I can't hold my urine anymore," she said without warning.

Growling, I squeezed the steering wheel of my delivery truck. "Come on, Connor. You can't wait?"

"Daddy, you know what holding urine can do to a growing urinary tract?"

"Spell it," I teased.

"Then you'll take me somewhere that has seat covers and soap. Not like the last time," Connor recapped, hopping around in her seat.

Laughing, I double-checked my route sheet to see where we were headed after driving around for too long aimlessly.

"Ms. Peach Street," I grumbled under my breath.

"Ms. Peach Street? Is she one of your girlfriends? Most importantly, can I use her restroom?"

"Hell no, she's not my girlfriend. She's a customer. Her delivery is next. I'm going to see if she's going to be an asshole today," I griped.

Adjusting the volume of the radio, Connor cut her eyes. "She must not be your type."

"Tuh. What's my type smart ass?" I wondered. After all the

shit I'd talked to Ciara, I was curious to know what Connor thought of the company I kept; even if she hardly had a preview.

Giggling, the princess who was too smart for her own good, filled her high cheekbones with air and puckered her lips out to resemble a duck. Slipping two small boxes under her Superwoman graphic-tee, Connor tried to speak.

"This."

"What is *that*?" I snarled ignorantly, although I knew exactly what she was implying.

"You know, like the girls on TV or the ones on Instagram," she explained.

Cutting my eyes, I asked. "Did your mama tell you that," I grimaced, parking on mean ass' street.

"No. Just because I don't have an Instagram doesn't mean I don't know what they look like on there."

"Yeah, well you're wrong. I think all women are beautiful. And daddy doesn't date women solely based on their physical appearance."

"Just their marital status," she blurted, then covered her mouth.

"Yeah, that was definitely outside of a child's place. Watch it, Connor," I chastised. I knew for a fact Connor had gotten that much from her mother. If Ciara had nothing else to hold over my head, my having relations with married women was it.

"Look, when we get up there, let me do all the talking," I warned.

Staring out the window, Connor whined. "Wow, look at her house."

"Connor! Did you hear me?"

"Kind of," she replied, her small voice wrapped in amusement. My groaning was enough of a sign to show I was serious.

Once on the porch I'd visited more times than I'd expected, I did what I knew was needed to make the homeowner speak. There wasn't a doubt in my mind she'd already seen us walk up.

"Good afternoon," I said into the intercom.

"Here we go again," she groaned, her heavy breath weighing on the line. "And you brought back up this time around I see."

The sudden lightness in her speech was evident since her usual hostility had rapidly gone ghost.

"I don't come here to fight you. I respect your rules and appreciate your business," I chimed meaning every word.

Giggling, the faceless woman cleared her throat dramatically. I knew she was having a field day with my humbling nature.

"Well Mr. Hollis, I appreciate your apology."

"That wasn't an— "

"Daddy!" Connor shrieked, cutting off my defense. I knew if I didn't hold my composure there was no chance she'd let us in.

"Ight. Ight. Now that we've gotten that out the way. I need a favor," I hurried to say.

"Excuse you?"

Bypassing her astonishment, I rattled off my request. "My little girl has to pee— "

"Daddy!" Connor objected poking me in the side.

"My bad. She has to use the ladies' room. I need you to allow her to use yours."

The stillness covering the porch made me join Connor in her two-step. I was restless and this new, unexpected, stoic temperament was disconcerting.

"Hello? Ms. Peach Street?" Connor blurted, sticking her round face in the obvious camera. Quickly, I pulled her back.

"No," the hiding hoarder said, finally issuing a reply.

"No?" my daughter and I countered in harmony.

"That's what I said."

Refusing to give up, Connor challenged her. "Aww, come on. You would really let a young girl hold her urine in place of kindness?"

–"I'm not letting a young girl do anything. Your daddy shouldn't have you outside totting boxes in the first place. I mean, I can be a killer for goodness sakes. You're willing to risk it all to prevent a UTI that may never come?" Peach Street inquired. I could tell by the way her tone changed; her answer was about to as well.

"Yes ma'am," Connor surrendered. We stood there for almost a minute without a mumbling word spilling through the speaker. Right as I got ready to have Connor go whizz on the side of her house, I heard door locks unlatch.

The door hadn't completed agape and the scent of peppermint had already found my nostrils. I was speechless when I finally laid eyes on the woman, I'd had on my mind for more than one reason. I wanted to laugh, scream and touch her all at the same time. She looked nothing like I envisioned over the last two months yet was exactly how I remembered her from Kennedy's baby shower.

Laughing inwardly, I purposely looked her up and down.

"Really. *Kross*?"

Ignoring me, she spoke to a grinning Connor. "The restroom is that first door past the kitchen. My dog may be in there but trust me, she won't bother you. Use it and come right back," she instructed. When I took a step to follow Connor, Kross pressed her small hand firmly in the center of my chest.

"No! She can go alone. No one else is—," she started, but caught herself. Even without her saying it, I knew Kross lived alone.

"She's a big girl. She *will* go by herself," she repeated more final this time. Looking to me for assurance, I told Connor to go and come back. Once I could no longer see her, I gave my attention to Kross.

"Why'd you act like you didn't know me?" I acknowledged, still stunned that weeks ago I laid eyes on the infamous Ms. Peach Street and wasn't aware. Just like before her short hair was in a fit of curls at the top, shorter on the sides accented by three stones lining her ears. Kross' upper body was hidden under an extra-large Nipsey Blue crew neck that read *Crenshaw;* her bottom barely consoled in biker shorts that stopped at her knees. The only difference from before was that she now wore glasses that added a studious undertone to her classic presence. I thought it was cute as hell how small her nose was and curved on the end.

"I don't know you," she answered being nonchalant. Aside from acting like she didn't care about being busted, the pretty lady could barely stop looking at me.

"Why'd you lie, Kross? I knew from the moment you opened your mouth at the baby shower, we'd shared the same space before."

"I didn't lie because you don't know me, Hollis. We talk crap while you deliver my packages. Sometimes it's funny, other times just annoying. That's it, that's all."

Scoffing, I looked passed her and into her home. From where I stood, I could see the scatter of papers and writing supplies aligning a wood coffee table and the sharp tenor of BB King caught my attention.

"Yeah? Something in my spirit doesn't believe that," I finally replied.

"Well, your spirit isn't the holiest, so let's not allow that to be an anchor for disaster," she jested, still delivering her witty comebacks. Now, seeing her bright smile accompanying the vibe had me damn near drooling.

"All done. Thank you again, Ms. Peach" Connor interrupted rejoining us.

"You're very welcome, beautiful. And you can call me, Kross."

"Got it. One more thing. I probably shouldn't have looked but your guitar is really cool. The all black with gold stars is really nice," Connor insinuated, overly excited.

"It's fine. You should have your dad put you in lessons," Kross implied with a sneaky smirk that Connor mimicked.

"Hmm, I feel like I'm about to get played, so we're about to head out," I announced, though my expression matched theirs.

"Thanks for looking out, Kross."

Fluffing Connor's two puffballs, Kross winked. "It's cool. She got me with the *"Ms. Peach Street"* thing," Kross admitted. I was surprised at how good I felt seeing them fawn over one another. Any other time, I would've called it ass kissin'.

After a formal goodbye we were back in the truck. Connor's seatbelt wasn't fastened before she was raving about the short hair beauty that had my head swimming since she opened the door. Kross knew exactly who I was from the day of Kennedy's event and continued to keep the charade going. Now, I wondered why.

"She's pretty, daddy," Connor mentioned googly eyed.

Nodding I agreed. "Yep."

"You should make her one of your girls."

I snarled at her impression of me. "I don't have girls; I have friends and Kross isn't one of them."

"Good, because I have a feeling, she's *thee* girl. You know they're different from the rest and trust me Daddy, after trying tomatoes after years of denying myself, I can confirm different can be really good."

CHAPTER Five

KROSS

 So, I have a new obsession. I don't mind speaking on it because hell, I'm proud! It gives my life substance, adds clarity to my days and pushes me to dig deeper. Her name is Snoh Aalegra. If you haven't heard of this gem, you're depriving yourself of some good shit! The Sweden songstress dropped her highly anticipated follow up album, 'uugh, in my feels again' less than a few months ago, and I've been hooked ever since. Her latest release provides all components required when deciding to submerge yourself in good vibes and energy only a good lyricist can provide. Though most addicts (like myself) are fawning over the new 12 list of conscious touching joints; one of my favorites from Ms. Aalegra has to be 'Walls', produced on her first LP. The thirty-two-year-old is set to get the world hooked on the purest melodies this fall in her first national tour! Y'all know if I mentioned Ms. lady, it's a vibe! Be sure to follow Snoh on all social media handles (dropped below) and check out her site for concert dates and tickets.

 Considering she has over 2 million monthly listeners on Spotify alone, I know I'm not the only one stuck in my feels!

 A sense of euphoria swept over me as it often did when I completed a write up for the Cali Buzz. I'd been writing for the state paper for nearly five years and outside of my jewelry creations, Kross Vibez was my creative offering to the world. I started dabbling with writeups while in high school and never lost the passion. The gig barely paid but thanks to social media and my thorough yet opinionated reviews on everything related to music, the job had somehow become lucrative. I had record companies more than once send demos my way to gather my opinion. Although I'd been playing the bass guitar since I was five and could actually hold a note in the vocal department, I never wanted to be the person behind the music, only the pen.

Reading over my latest spill I smiled knowing the root of the article was planted by a man I couldn't stop thinking about. Hollis Brown had been a fixate in my brain since popping up on my doorstep with his pretty princess. She was a splitting image of a mother I wondered about with remnants of her father. Hollis openly flirted but that didn't mean he wasn't taken, just meant he was a flirt. Sadly, his quick wit and playful jabs were enough to make me mention him to Dr. Sway. I didn't share more than I knew but I also didn't hide my wonder. Roland left a bitter taste in my mouth but it wasn't enough to curve my curiosity when it came to Hollis. I prayed my inquisitiveness didn't kill the cat; I had about cashed in on my nine lives.

Rolling my eyes, I saw my father was the one responsible for my phone ringing off the hook. I knew he'd heard about what happened at Kennedy's baby shower and was calling me for details. Since my inclusion began the relationship between my parents and I hadn't been as tight as it once was. My mom blamed me for sneakily bringing drama into the brothel, whereas my dad was just disappointed. There was a process to become a client at *Body* and since I was being selfish, Porter hadn't gon' through the usual background check. If he had, his publicly problematic wife would've been enough to reject him.

"Hey daddy," I answered, putting my best happy voice in effect.

"Hey, beautiful. I hear someone's finally feeling better. Been out and about, huh?"

"Yeah, something like that."

"That's good to hear. When do you think you'll be coming

back to work? We could use an accountant," he shared like I gave a shit. My dad knew I hated the numbers gig. I only did it because my mother trained me on how to balance the books and they kept reiterating that this was *our* family business. Deciding not to pacify the station, I spoke candidly.

"Daddy, I almost died in that place. I suffer from PTSD and you want me to go to the specific location that triggers my anxiety," I recognized aloud, noticing how foul it sounded.

"I think you're much stronger than you're giving yourself credit for, Kross. You're a woman. You're built to struggle and boss up to resilience. You've been around *this* life, your entire life, you know the game that's why you jumped into it. Don't pretend to be better than your family," he yelled.

"I'm not trying to be better than anyone except my old self and for some reason that offends people. I'm learning to be strong, but guess what? Strong isn't easy for everybody! Walking away after the fire would've made you stronger in my eyes, not taking money to rebuild the place that holds my nightmares, daddy."

"Your mother and I treated you like a princess, you chose to decrease to the level of the peasants. We can't shut down rotation because you got out of line. We didn't do it for your brother, what makes you think we'd do it for you?"

"Bye, Dad," I replied hanging up in his face. It took everything for me not to cry out. I was used to hearing the sternness melt from his tone, just not directed at me. My dad could be childish and menacing when pushed so I knew he was probably in his feelings because I went to Kennedy before seeing him once I decided to reemerge. He and my brother treated me like divorced parents who couldn't get along but had to co-parent. Everyone wanted to be the favorite.

Following Daisy's barks, I found her in her favorite spot. Unlike most times, she was going crazy over something apparently under my bathroom sink.

"Hey. Hey. Stop making all that noise," I chastised. Checking the area she had motioned towards, I opened the cabinet to find a vibrating cell phone placed directly next to an unopened box of Tampons.

"What do we have here?" I examined, pressing the power button on the side. My heart dropped when a photo of Connor and her father brightened the screen.

"That little devil," I recited, recalling the sneaky smirk on Connor's face when she came out my bathroom during their quick visit.

All giddy and hyper, I rushed to the living room completely forgetting the disagreement I'd just had with my dad.

Flopping down on my love seat, I got to work. Like a mischievous nerd, I closely studied the screen of the phone with one eye closed while the other narrowed. Following the smudges riddled across the face, I followed the pattern twice before the phone unlocked.

"Bingo!" I praised, twerking a little in my seat.

"What?" I asked innocently, catching the funny look Daisy gave me.

"Uh. Uh. Don't give me that look. You're supposed to be on my side, girl."

Catching my drift, my blue-eyed pit leaped onto the cushion beside me and snuggled her head against my thigh. For nearly twenty minutes, I snooped through what appeared to be Hollis' work phone. Outside of the screen saver that held a picture of Connor, there wasn't much personal information to be found. Until... I reached his messages. Once I opened the text app, I saw exactly why he had been blowing up the lost phone like a crackhead; this was how he kept in touch with his hoes.

"Guess, he isn't all he was cracked up to be," I said aloud and smiled when Daisy growled. I thought to text a few of the women and pretend to be Hollis for fun but promptly ceded the idea. I could already tell Hollis had a hot temper and I didn't know these women's situations to go steering their pots. What I could gather from the late-night messages between them and Hollis was at least two of the three were married. The one name, *Shady Shelby* was serious about her Handsome Hollis. Laughing, I snooped until I damn near had a heart attack.

Startled, I almost dropped the phone when it began vibrating in my grasp. Seeing *Boss* flash across the screen had my already quickly pacing heart to increase its speed. I don't know why I was nervous about answering when I knew for certain it was Hollis calling.

"Hello," I answered after listening to him breathe on the line without forming actual words.

"Aye. Who the hell is this? And where is my phone?" he blurted.

Pulling the device from my ear, I snarled. "You shouldn't be so careless with your belongings, maybe then you'd know where they are, homewrecker."

All of a sudden, the line went quiet as it had previously. I knew his mind was on my callous name-calling.

"Kross?"

"Yep. Your phone was going crazy under my bathroom sink. Don't ask me how it got there because I don't know. You're welcome to come to get it tomorrow," I concluded, not fond of how I actually wanted to invite him over tonight. I hadn't had a man in my house since Roland left nine months ago and honestly we didn't have the most affectionate memories. I didn't want a repeat of that confusion.

"Why can't I come tonight? We don't live far from one another," Hollis made it a point to reveal.

"That means nothing. I'm not Ivory, Sam or Shelby," I reminded him, mentioning the names I saw on his phone. "You can't pull up on me when you see fit. You can come pick it up tomorrow or how about I mail it to you," I proffered sarcastically.

Like he'd found a clue, Hollis laughed loud enough for me to hear. "I see what's going on here."

Ignorantly, I asked him to elaborate.

"You're jealous. You went searching and now you're pissed you found exactly what you were looking for. That's not on me and considering I'm not committed to anyone, I don't have to explain shit you saw."

"I don't remember asking you, foo'. Nothing that I've read was a surprise other than learning you prefer your women seasoned and committed," I spat, compromising the cool I was trying to maintain.

"You're saying a lot for someone who went through my shit. I should press charges on yo ass."

"With everything else revealed tonight, learning you're a snitch wouldn't be a total shock," I trolled.

Amongst a menacing chuckle, Hollis found his words. "Screw you, Kross."

"Come on, you know I'm way out of your age bracket," I clowned, my laugh filing the line and colliding with the dial tone.

"Wow, someone's in their feelings tonight."

CHAPTER *Six*

HOLLIS

"If I told you that you couldn't come over last night, why would you think tonight would suffice? I said during the day."

"Listen, I just worked a thirteen-hour shift, I on-boarded four new customers and Connor is driving me crazy practicing for this recital, be nice. For once," I requested waiting for Kross to open the door.

Instead of giving me her usual pushback, her steel protector adjourned and shifted my bad day to better. Her smile served as a welcome mat for my presence even in the scope of her complaints. Kross was dressed for bed but her upbeat nature suggested otherwise. Nothing other than a few cars roaming the neighborhood added sound to the street, light post stood tall illuminating our subtle stance. Neither of us made a move, just stared awaiting some type of action from the other. Any move, word or even some combative insult would've made me more comfortable than the calm. The smoothness was unfamiliar.

"Can I come inside this time or do I have to wait out here again?" I asked exhausted from the day's event. I hated how my days had become filled with more tension, more often.

Instead of replying, Kross stepped to the side. I tried not to react when her breasts brushed against my arm as I entered. Three steps into the honeycomb hideout and my eyes scattered, taking in how dope her home was. Swiftly, my concentration landed on the chessboard resting in the center of a wide table.

"Let's play?"

Cautiously, Kross walked towards me. "Hmm, I don't know. Don't you want your phone first? Don't you have to get back to Connor?"

"The phone isn't going anywhere. Connor is with my family and I'm where I need to be," I told her, not grasping how intimate the statement sounded until her impression confirmed that sentiment.

"I'm not going to do anything to you, Kross," I affirmed, sighting the nervousness in her face. I had a long day and needed a stress reliever; she was going to help me, nothing more, nothing less.

"I'm not afraid of you doing anything to me. If you try it, my dog will eat your tall ass alive," she acknowledged, moving over to the couch opposite of where I sat without permission.

"I'm not worried about *you* or *your dog*. Get the pieces together and let's play, stalling ain't gon' stop me from whippin' yo ass," I joked, removing my bomber jacket and making myself comfortable.

"Ha! Unlike you, I don't need any favors. You two in the hole partna'. First, I helped out with your kid, and now your phone," she reminded me. "Would you like something to drink? I have Henny, Jose Cueva, wine."

"Water is coo'."

Shock registered on her round face at my reply. "You don't drink?"

"Not unless we're celebrating," I advised, trying not to stare at feet I noticed were pretty as hell when she opened the door for Connor and I weeks ago. Between a woman's feet and legs, I don't know which I found most breathtaking. And ironically tonight, Kross had both on display. I noticed how Kross was buoyant when it came to baring skin, but the opposite otherwise.

In a lighter voice, Kross nodded with a grin that may not have been meant for me, but I enjoyed witnessing.

"A person with restraint is a very rare thing. You should be proud. That doesn't mean I'm not still going to pour a full cup of Stellar Rose, but," she paused as if hearing her rambling.

"It's good to know," she concluded.

"That's not the only thing good about me, Kross."

Pointing to the board, she waved me off. "Yeah, we're about to see how true that is."

Two hours later, and almost two games in the hole, Kross and I hadn't realized it was close to ten until Connor called to say goodnight. My sister offered for her to stay the night with her and my mom after I mentioned my hectic schedule for the day.

Making her move, Kross shuffled the appropriate piece in the path of my pawn. She was careful and more strategic in her movement than I'd expected from her.

"Who named you?" I asked out of the blue.

"My father. He always says from the moment my mom announced she was having a girl, he knew I was worthy to be praised, so he named me Kross," she admitted, never removing her eyes from the chessboard.

"That's deep. Narcissistic as fuck, but I guess it makes sense. The way you talk about him and all that quick wordplay has the ole g sounding like a pimp."

"That's because he is. Checkmate," she announced before I could identify what was happening. The way Kross rotated her small hips in her seat made me care less about losing. The desire of winning left the moment she answered the door in a white beater that gave a clear preview to pierced nipples. A woman who sought out pain was dangerous.

"You serious about what you said?"

Her full eyebrows shot up.

"Don't look at me like that. It's not like you've said much. What you said about your dad, is it true?"

Sitting back, Kross folded her legs so they were tucked under her butt. "I mean that's not the type of profession you lie about."

"Depends on who you're talking to," I replied.

"Let's play two truths and a lie," she abruptly proposed to shift the temperature.

"You just gon' change the subject like that?"

Her reply was a toothless grin.

"Always with the games," I chuckled. "Ok. You go first."

"I bet," she scoffed, her brown, cat shaped eyes looking up towards the string of Christmas lights decorating her roof. Kross' home was draped like the inside of an IKEA catalog. Everything from her tweed pattern furniture to the porch swing in the inside of her home.

"I'm scared of the dark. I love to cook. I used to work in a brothel," she answered, grinning impishly.

"Considering you have lights all-around your house and you're thick in the right places, I'd say the first two are facts, last is the lie. I know your ass didn't work in a hoe house regardless of what you said about your Pops."

Shaking her head, Kross exhaled loudly. "You're wrong, Hollis. I've actually been around those types of places most of life. Your turn."

"Nah, go back."

"Nah, keep going. It's your turn."

Not wanting to continue, but knowing it was only fair, I spoke my truth.

"I've been to the pen. I've never been in a real relationship cause these hoes ain't loyal. I don't have any tattoos," I revealed.

Giggling, Kross started to squirm. "Your negative energy about being involved is real, so I'll say you're a criminal and like pain. I've seen your tattoos."

"I'm not the only one, Ms. Nipple Rings and Brothel."

"Don't go there," she groaned, her tone uplifting. Feeling the calm slip from beneath us start to depart, I figured it was time to head out.

"It's getting late. I appreciate you returning the phone. Trust me, I'm going to kick Connor's ass for being—"

"Like you?" she interjected, a toothless smirk taking place of her curvy lips. Laughing, I headed towards the door.

"Wait," Kross' raspy voice called out behind me. Without turning to face her, my steps ceased.

"What's up?"

"You...want to watch a movie or something?" The awkwardness in her invitation premiered in her tone.

"Tell me you want me to stay first," I challenged. I was already within arm's reach of her door, could've left if I wanted to, but something kept me still. I knew Kross would keep beating around the bush if I let her. Every time I asked a question, she kept everything vague. Usually, I appreciated the privacy, but with Kross I wanted to know everything. My main reason for being here had slipped away before I stepped through the door.

"I'm not saying that," she shrieked, chinky eyes gravitating to the hardwood floor.

"Ok. Bye."

"Bye," she replied hastily. I peered over my shoulder to see the coffee with one shot of cream-colored woman gathering the chess pieces we'd just used.

"You're still here," she noted, glaring up from her task.

"You're one difficult lady."

Quickly, she abandoned the things in her grasp and crossed her arms. Her body facing me gave easy access to everything on the outside that made her beautiful. From her tone legs that looked like she'd been running track her entire life, to the length of her neck that resembled a gorgeous swan. Hell, even Kross' shut off nature was enticing. I was used to women being easy, I was like a dog in heat in the company of a goddess with self-discipline.

"I'm not difficult Hollis, you're greedy. I invite you to stay, but that's not good enough."

"Me asking for clearer terms is me being greedy? You wanting a person to jump through hoops to connect with you is greedy. You don't get to tell me the things you've been through and think I won't dig deeper!"

"And yet, you still haven't left," she chimed in a sarcastic sneer. Her hardness only held for moments before her juicy lips balled.

"Stop pouting. If you stop being stubborn, you would have some company. I know you're tired of sitting in this cage talking to yourself."

Scowling, Kross took precise steps to where I stood.

"I don't know where we got off wrong but I'm not desperate for anyone's attention or company. If you don't want to stay, leave. You don't even know me but want to control how much of me I show you."

"If you'd wasted as much time on getting to know people as I have, you'd understand my approach."

"Had you been more transparent about that in the first place, I would have respected that," she debated, her arms slowly descending to her sides.

"You gon' respect it now," I retorted, smirking at her brass response. "You don't feel secure outside, so I came in. What you gon' do with me now because I'm not gon' fight you, woman."

Sealing glossed lips, the brown beauty, shook her head. The hint of sangria on her breath triggered my tongue to ran across my own lips.

"I can feed you?" Her cat cut orbs, widened. "Wait, that didn't sound right. What I meant was—"

"Exactly what you said," I threw in. I didn't want Kross to correct herself. I wanted the roaming thought of her feeding me pussy and pasta to twirl on her conscious.

"You like Flautas?"

"I don't know what the hell that is but it sounds Mexican and that's my favorite so, I'm sure it's straight."

"You don't really have much of a choice. That's like the only thing I can cook without burning down the house," she admitted, leading me to her kitchen.

"Your mom didn't teach you how to cook?" I asked innocently.

"Not in the kitchen," she replied seductively rather she knew it or not.

"Skylight is nice," I pointed out, switching subject while admiring the accent of her home.

"Yeah, when I started... staying to myself. Kennedy insisted on installing the opening. Said I needed some light in my darkness."

Frowning at my reaction, Kross nodded her head. "What's funny?"

"You call your seclusion, "staying to yourself", that's funny."

"What would you call it?" she questioned, walking backward down her hallway.

"Hiding."

"Yeah, but that would mean I was afraid. Everyone thinks I stay in the house because I'm afraid of dying after the fire and shooting," she recalled, forgetting I didn't know the whole story.

"After what I've been through, Hollis, I'm not afraid of dying."

Nodding, I agreed with Kross. "Oh, I know. You're afraid of living."

～ Giving me her back, I asked Kross to tell me what made her a prisoner in her own home. I wanted to know why she was afraid of the dark. However, instead of sharing, she demanded I grab the milk from the refrigerator and add a record to her vinyl player.

"It's a long story that I'd not ready to get into. Just know, I survived even when people I thought I knew, relationships I had, and pain I lived through almost took me out. People judge what they don't know, so I get your curiosity. Just trust that when I feel safe enough I'll tell you anything you want to know, just like when you share the details of your bid it'll be on your terms," she professed, cleaning vegetables she was seconds from chopping. Watching Kross and feeling my head lighten at just the visual of her was also a reminder that I had to get the shit with Shelby in order. I didn't know where things were going, but either way

Shelby couldn't be a factor. Kross' past was already a big enough hurdle.

Initially, I contemplated googling the incident versus pulling teeth from Kross to be more transparent. Something in my moral compass wasn't okay with that move now. I wanted to know Kross because she invited me into her sanctuary, not because I invaded her privacy. Maybe then, she'd stay.

CHAPTER Seven

KROSS

Dressed in black leggings, my favorite 'Black Power' crew neck, and colorful tube socks, I slowly stepped onto my porch with my guitar in one hand and Daisy on my heels. It was almost time for lunch and shockingly, I appreciated the light traffic and few folks littering the streets. After finishing up my piece for the Cali Buzz, I was feigning for fresh air. Since the first time out, natural air had become a new necessity of mine.

Removing my left Air Pod from its post, I slipped the piece into my ear. On impact the deep tone of H.E.R that I had on pause glided through the small speaker.

Humming the soft melody, my fingers moved naturally over the guitar strings completely removing me from my physical position. Heavy doubt oozed from my core and melted on the pavement, as the lyrics to 'Going' faded into my spirit.

"I've been going, I've been going, I've been focused. Just be with me at the moment. Trust me I know how you feel right now, baby that's just what it is right now. Just stay with me, right behind you and I'm trying to, make the time to. Baby that's all I can give right now."

Singing a few additional lines of the song, and freestyling on my favorite instrument I paused when I felt someone watching me.

"Damn, she's pretty," I heard someone comment in the middle of my verbal mediation. Lifting my lids one at a time, I almost choked on my own spit seeing I had an audience standing at the bottom of the three steps leading to my door.

A thin smirk that matched mine covered Kennedy's face. He always wore this proud expression when watching me in my element. When I concentrated on who he'd brought along with him, my grin descended. I wasn't upset with the man's presence, just surprised. It had been a week since our random dinner and chess game.

Avoiding his trained attention, I looked to Kennedy for clarity.

"Hmm, what are you doing here?" Covering my legs with the plaid throw blanket I'd brought outside with me, I squirmed thinking of what my hair may have looked like and prayed I didn't have pieces off pecan pie crust stuck to my chin. Though I worked from home, most days I tried to look half decent. Today wasn't one of those days.

When neither man spoke, I set my guitar to the side and waved my hand dramatically. "Hello?"

Taking the lead, Hollis came closer. His eyes shifted between my face and the guitar he'd just gotten a free listen of. It had been long enough but my heart was still moving like Gail Devers on the track, at their abrupt visit.

"That was dope as hell," Hollis proposed. I could see the astonishment on his face and refused to show how good it made me feel.

"You can't just pop up at my house."

Groaning, Kennedy inched up the stairs.

"I don't need a reason to come and see my sister," he griped, avoiding eye contact. "Hollis is training me on the morning shift and thankfully, your house is a part of his route."

Tilting my head to the side, my brows dipped. "Thankfully?"

"Well, we have something for you and I gotta take a shit," he revealed in a murmur.

"Aht. Aht. Not in my house you don't. I'm sure you still use too much toilet paper and not enough soap," I complained, standing to my feet. I tried to ignore how Hollis blatantly eyed me just like he had at the baby shower.

"Catch," Kennedy shouted.

Raising my hand, I caught the small box he'd tossed with little warning.

"Damn Kennedy, I'm happy I didn't have anything that could break inside of here. If this is what you're going to do with packages, please stay working the night shift."

Opening the box, I grinned from ear to ear knowing exactly what was inside under the stock paper and receipts.

"Shut up. Hollis gimme ten minutes."

"Kennedy," I urged.

"You have two big ass bathrooms. Don't be selfish, girl," he called out, already disappearing in my house.

"What the hell? This isn't a damn one-stop," I complained, lowering my tone

Feeling *his* attention, I toyed with the box in my grip. Just the thought of *him* overwhelmed my conscious, my doubts and every other part of me that couldn't measure the value in getting to know him.

"You could've given me a heads up," I randomly stated, returning to where my guitar rested on the cute loveseat settled on my porch for decoration. Instead of sitting beside me, the giant set on the top step of my porch. For once I was looking down at him instead of the other way around.

"I tried to tell you but you didn't pick up. Now I see why," he declared, pointing towards my guitar, pen, and paper.

"What are you working on."

Holding my chest, I squealed. "Excuse you, my business."

"Didn't you tell me you're a published writer? You know I could just google it." Deciding not to be difficult, I spoke as candidly as my conscious would allow.

"I'm working on a new piece for my column. And considering I haven't heard from you in a week, you shouldn't be concerned."

"I had to get some shit straight before making you my girlfriend. What's the topic?" he demanded to know.

Instead of pushing Hollis on his disappearing act or falling for his sweet talk, I shared. "The beauty of interludes. I mention some of my favorites and I offer a playlist I compiled for my readers. I never understood why artist decide to make some of their most noteworthy lyrics apart of an incomplete body of work."

Shrugging, Hollis randomly pulled a wrapped peach from his baggy cargo pants. Biting into fruit I couldn't detach my eyes from, Hollis continued with his suggestion.

"I hope you have Justin Timberlake's, 'Set the Mood' on there."

"That's a prelude, but you get a pass," I hinted, wrinkling my nose bashfully. I knew I looked like a damn fool with my mouth faintly opening every time Hollis' set of perfect white teeth clashed into the orange fruit.

"What you know about JT?" I asked struggling to keep my cool intact. When Hollis looked from his snack to me and laughed, I got the impression he'd picked up on my uncensored thinking.

"I know he's a dope artist who has one of the smoothest interludes," he repeated, still eating that damn peach-like it was a part of the last supper. Though I watched his lips move, my senses were stuck on the juice Hollis let leaked from the corners of his lips before sopping up the stream up with a napkin.

Mischievously, the chocolate specimen taunted me. "You want a bite?"

"Yes," I answered breathlessly. "Wait. No. No!"

"Too late, you already said yes."

Flustered, I crossed my arms over my chest doing my best to appear serious despite the humor Hollis had obviously found in the situation.

Resting his elbows on top of his knees, the arrogant man looked over at me. "Nah, it's coo'. Regardless of what your mouth said, your eyes answered on your behalf. This isn't the first time either but I'll give you time to feel comfortable asking for what you want. And to answer your question, I listen to all types of music. I'm not as one-sided as you may think."

"After speaking to you on the phone for a few days before you went ghost, I learned enough to know that's true." I paused. "On the other hand, just like you were shocked I didn't look like Flavor Fav behind my door, I have the right to be surprised you listen to something other than Mozzy and J-Cole. It's refreshing. Ever think of getting into some arena of music?"

Hollis shook his head. "I just like to listen. I mean other than owning Brown Brothas, I thought of boxing. Could never control my temper long enough to master the technical shit."

"I was always told, a man who has no control has no power."

"In that case, I could definitely do better," he admitted his attention moving to the passing traffic. After too much silence, Hollis gave me his eyes again. I had never taken mine off him.

"You're beautiful, Kross."

"You've been telling me that since the first time you laid eyes on me but is it enough?" I questioned jokingly.

Straightening his posture, Hollis squared his shoulders. "It is for now. What's in the box?" he ordered, disconnecting the heavy of where our conversation was headed.

Refocusing completely on the box I clenched in my lap, I bounced around in my seat seeing my new guitar pick inside.

"Yes! Yes!" I squealed, admiring the pick I ordered.

"You only play for yourself or do you let other people in on your gift. And I'm not talking about your neighbors that get a free show every now and again."

"Hmm, it's a personal thing. Amongst other...things my mom taught me how to play the bass over twenty years ago. And no, I don't play professionally. It's for my sanity."

"Well, you may need to share some of that calm with me. Shit is crazy and solace is always welcomed," he stated, again focusing on the cars passing us by.

"Gotta find that within, Hollis."

"You too selfish to share yours with me?"

"No, I'm too mindful to lose it in exchange for nothing."

Smiling, Hollis stood then joined my side. The bright colored sofa clashed with his dark skin, triggering my eyes to dance over his coating.

Snickering, Hollis waved a finger. "Oh, so there *is* something worth your sanity."

"That's not what I meant, but I guess…yeah. Love could be worth my sanity. Love takes you outside of your own rationale. Makes you sacrifice and compromise elements of yourself that are unfathomable. The person you're exchanging your rationality for should be giving something that can fill the void of what you're surrendering. The person should mean more than the discomfort. Get me?"

"I think I do," he replied. The feeling of his finger touching my chin prompted my body to loosen.

"Now, stop being stingy. I want to hear you play. You didn't get a new pick for nothing."

"Pull it up on YouTube, nigga. I warned you about my sister," Kennedy announced, stepping out with fried chicken in one hand and a biscuit in the other.

Clearing his height by almost a foot, Hollis matched Kennedy's posture. "And I already told you. You're her brother, not her daddy and even then, you can't tell me what this woman needs."

Sliding down in my seat, I recoiled at their bantering. Trying hard not to tell Kennedy to carry on with his day and invite Hollis inside, I spoke up. "Excuse you. I am sitting right here. Take that catfight off my porch."

Winking, Hollis slightly pinched my chin once more before walking off.

"Stop looking at that man like you know him. Hollis ain't for you, sis. Trust me."

Smiling sarcastically, I shooed him off, careful not to show any hint that his warning was a tad bit too late. No, Hollis and I weren't dating but I'd be lying if I said that's not where we were headed. Hell, had I listened to my intuition I'd be under the influence that we were going far beyond that.

"I'm serious about what I said, Kross."

"I know," I called out, uncaringly stealing glances at Hollis who leaned against the black truck with his focus trained on me. Kennedy cut his eyes at our interaction. He knew at the end of the day Hollis was the boss and personal matters needed to be yielded while on the clock. Things were different for Hollis because his name was the one on the big black trucks making deliveries all over town.

My brother had a difficult time allowing me the freedom to make my own mistakes and sadly, his hovering is what kept me at bay. Honestly, Kennedy's coverage was fair notice that I had something to be afraid of. Nevertheless, I felt butterflies erupt at the mere notion that Hollis didn't give a damn about my brother's protective demeanor or his protest. It was yet another thing the hot-tempered man and I had in common.

CHAPTER Eight

KROSS

"Are you sure you don't want me to go with you. Don't overexert your mental trying to prove a point. Besides, I could use the exercise right about now," Truth empathized, though it was too late. I was already on my second lap around my block and headed back in the direction of my home. I woke up early with more ambition to feel more of a breeze than I'd felt in a while. I didn't want a chaperone this go around.

"I'm already on the move and I have Daisy with me but I appreciate your offering. I'm really tired of feeling like a burden, even if you don't agree."

Sighing, Truth's worry seeped through the line rather she knew it or not. Wanting to liven up her mood, I decided to share my subtle news.

"I've been talking to a boy," I giggled, my snickering growing louder at her catty cheering.

"Hmm, and I'm pretty sure I know who that is. Does your brother know you've been talking to his boss?"

Snarling, I cautioned my annoyance. I knew Truth was only asking out of concern. I hadn't kept time with a man who wasn't family in a while and my last situation didn't end well. Roland left when I thought I needed him most. The night terrors, quiet spells and my apprehensive narrative was too much for him to love me through. Kennedy, Truth and everyone else who cared was pissed at his decision to walk away when I couldn't distinguish what was important versus what I'd experienced.

"I haven't said anything to Kennedy because there's nothing more to tell other than what I just said. We've been talking," I reiterated, chilling a hyper Daisy. Her movements prompted me to check my back.

"Hey, don't let my prying downplay your excitement. I'm not questioning you, was just asking a question, Kross," she urged. Knowing I had no one else to share my butterfly episodes with, I disclosed what I'd been thinking.

"He's so coo', Truth'. He's thirty-one, single, and a business owner. He's also funny as hell. I met his daughter a few weeks ago when she had to use the restroom while working with him for the day. He's nothing like Roland, and I appreciate that," I murmured, grateful for that fact. Roland was great when serving his purpose in *Body* but once the place went up in flames, so did our relationship.

"Did Hollis have a fit when he saw you were the same chick from the shower. He wasn't lying when he said he knew your scheming ass," she accused snickering.

"He pressed me about it but it was short-lived. Honestly, I didn't want to scare him away. I know my reputation around Colten, the city isn't that big. If I would've revealed who I was on the spot he may have...I don't know," I stumbled, not wanting to admit I was leery about running another man away with my issues. Issues even I could confess were hard to tolerate.

"Don't do that. Any man blessed enough to call you his own is getting a woman who has a story to tell. You're beautiful, goal-orientated and you have a good heart. These niggas have no room to judge," Truth defended, my brother's voice interrupting our girl talk.

"Who the hell y'all talking about?"

I rolled my eyes at his pestering. Kennedy was only two years older than me but acted like my daddy whenever given the chance.

"None of your business. Get back," Truth snickered. I sensed in her tone, she wanted to play with her man. Seeing the FaceTime request from Hollis pop onto my screen pushed me to end the call even faster.

Slowing my stride, I smoothed down my hair. Releasing a deep exhale, I slid the answer button over to connect a call I was looking forward to.

"Hey," I answered, surprised at who was on the line.

"Good morning, Ms. Kross. I know you're probably wondering why I'm calling but I had a question," Connor said, straightening the collar of what appeared to be a uniform shirt. She looked adorable with her hair braided in two Pocahontas style straight backs, and her ears glistening with small gold hoops.

"Good morning, Connor. Shoot," I responded, entertaining the nerve she'd worked up to call me. Frankly, I may have been more nervous than she was.

Getting comfortable on a bed, Connor grinned. "So, I'm really interested in learning how to play the guitar and—"

Interjecting, I assumed the adult role before letting her continue. "Hmm, does your daddy know you face-timed me?"

"Hmm, I don't think so. He's in there stinking up the bathroom," she disclosed, a nonchalant shrug was the measurement of her concern.

"So, back to those lessons. You think you can teach me how to play the guitar?"

Uncertain of what to say, and not wanting to let her down, I decided to be honest. "I've never taught anyone how—"

"Doesn't mean you lack the ability to do so," Hollis' deep voice encouraged after he'd snatched the phone from Connor.

"Give it back," she squealed. I laughed seeing her jump on his shoulders trying to get it back.

Letting my vulnerable energy cloud our call, I probed. "Why are you invading our conversation? You didn't bother to call me, Connor did."

The crooked smile I had starting to adore softened my demeanor.

"Aww, you missed me. The last time we talked, you fell asleep on the phone and never called back."

Removing my eyes, I checked my surroundings once more as I entered my gate feeling accomplished, even for something trivial for most.

"I guess my snoring scared you off," I wondered aloud, knowing I sounded like an insecurity bird. It had only been two days since we spoke and being truthful, he didn't owe me anything.

"Nothing can scare me off, Kross," Hollis volunteered. Seconds later, he was clowning while pointing at the screen.

"Except for that hairline. You know I got my L's in the pen," he invited, baiting me to say yes. We'd shared a few phone conversations and enough for me to already know he'd been locked up for five years. That didn't sway my impression of him. The fact that he entertained women already taken versus finding one of his own was what kept me at a pause. Sadly, it didn't render a complete halt to the indescribable energy we exchanged.

"Boy please, I don't want no damn jailhouse cut," I teased, drinking a swig of bottled water. Flopping down on what I made out to be a recliner, Hollis refused to let up.

"Why not? Better than walking around with that baby afro puff on the side."

"Aww, Kross. You gon' let him talk to you like that?" Connor popped in to say, causing both her dad and me to laugh this time.

"I'm not worried about him. We both know I look better than his momma," I chimed, giving in to Connor's bantering. Giving her a wink, I titled my head shyly as Connor got excited. I kept trying to ignore the warmth I felt while speaking to them. I didn't want to get too in over my head that I forgot boundaries and the Scarlett letter on my chest.

"Don't start daydreaming now, I told you I don't bite. You looked out for us, let me return the favor," he proposed making it hard as hell to say no while offering bare-chested and chocolate coated.

Petting Daisy as we entered my front door, I rubbed her head and asked what she thought about Hollis' proposal. When she barked twice, I took that as a yes.

"Guess that's a yes," Hollis wondered, licking his lips like he could taste me through the lens.

Ignoring his expression, I checked my home before opening the mail I'd grabbed from the box.

Getting comfortable, I tuned back into the conversation.

"I guess, it couldn't hurt. When do you wanna do it?"

"Eww," Connor tutted.

"Get yo ass back, always in grown folks' business," Hollis chastised. "Go get your backpack. It's almost time for me to drop you at the plantation."

"Not with that breath and no shirt on it isn't," Connor broadcasted, giggling.

"Bye Kross! I'll call to set up my first lesson," the bold beauty yelled, running out the room as Hollis' threats followed behind her. Just like the relationship I shared with my dad, theirs was unconventional, but it worked.

"I gotta get her outta here. I'll see you tomorrow at around six. Coo'?" he asked, leaning into the frame. The moment my cheeks packed with yearning, I wished I could disappear. It was tragic that aside from how extremely liberal my home was growing up; I'd rarely had these types of moments with the opposite sex. I was taught to keep my mind on the business, and unless a man's pockets were laced, I didn't need him. That emotion didn't work for a woman who had her own.

"Tomorrow is fine, just be here before the sun sets please," I suggested, ending the call before my jaws went numb from smiling so much.

Kicking my feet like an untamed schoolgirl, I danced in my seat recalling how good close felt. Being so close, I could jump in his lap or on his face. I rejoiced thinking about a real man pouring into me something I'd denied myself of for so long.

Sighting an envelope in the stack that read *Vibez*, I quickly ripped it open. Upon reading the request enclosed, I damn near lost it.

"Yes!" I screamed, jolting Daisy from her meal.

"Sorry, baby," I cooed, rereading the letter. Someone was requesting ten-thousand dollars' worth of Vibez jewels. The check enclosed, along with the designs preferred, let me know it was real. Mid-praise, I frowned speculating how the client could have gotten my address. Most of my orders routed via Instagram or my website.

"Don't overthink it. There's a phone number, name and return address listed. They'd be a dumb ass criminal," I mumbled, staring at the check and its packaging.

"Just go with the flow, Kross and pray your intent counts for enough," I coached, hoping my intuition hadn't shrunk to nothing.

CHAPTER Nine

HOLLIS

"You really about to go kick it with the hermit, again. This is a new day for sure," Rock joked, elbowing me as we shut down the building for the night.

"Shut the hell up. Aren't you the one that's always preaching about how much I need to leave the married broads alone?" I asked.

"Yeah, but I didn't tell you to go lay up with the cat lady. This will be the third time you've been in her house and haven't said shit to Moses about the bet. I think you like it in the sunken place."

"Man, get on with that. Kross is actually coo' as fuck. She helped me out with Connor, so she's good in my book," I stressed.

Blowing out his worry, my cousin ran his hand down the length of his face.

"I just want you to be careful. As coo' as she may be, I know she got issues. I just don't want you taking on someone's else mess. I've watched you do that time and time again, and I don't want you hurt like before. You know it's all love," Rock stated.

"I hear you, and I'll remember that," I dismissed, dappin' him up and heading to my car. I was done with deliveries for the day and hoped Kross wasn't in her feelings when I got there. We'd finally settled on a day for me to put my clippers to her Jimmy Neutron and considering, I was an hour late, I knew there was a chance, I'd be left on her porch.

"Hollis! Hollis!" I heard someone call out as I opened the door.

"What the fuck are you doing here Shelby? I told you after that rundown at the Marriott, our thing is over," I recapped, getting ready to shut my door before she wedged her body in the space.

Rubbing her cold hands down my face, Shelby cried. "Baby, please. I know what you said, but I promise you don't have to worry about Henry. He's on the road again, so we'll have no interruptions. I know you miss me. You can't just throw me away, Hollis."

"Shelby, focus on your marriage and get some help. Stalking my moves, ain't gon' work in your favor. Worry about your man. It's obvious that nigga loves you," I professed, hardly recognizing my own advice.

"Love? He doesn't love me! Always on the road, doing God knows what while I'm home being a good little wife," she yelled in disgust. Considering, I fucked Shelby for nearly six months, I knew her statement was false.

"But that's what you signed up for! You said it yourself that man's always been the way he is. Love that him for who he is and stop tryna use me as a distraction from the shit I can't help you with," I barked. If I'd learned nothing during the time with my daughter and Kross, I learned patience was required in any relationship and Shelby wasn't giving her marriage a fair shot in my opinion.

Taking away Shelby's opportunity to stake her claim again, headlights flashed in our direction. I growled when I saw the same blue pickup from the Marriott easing into my business lot deliberately.

"Get that nigga off my property and get the hell on. I told you at the beginning of us messing around, I don't do drama. You from the gate you knew Henry worked for me, you were being messy! Stop acting desperate, Shelby before someone gets hurt," I advised, leaving her to face the man she'd vowed to love and respect.

Thirty minutes later, I pulled up to Kross' home and prepared myself for her confrontational temper. Normally, I shied away from women with the temperament, yet Kross gave the tough climate some allure.

"You're late," she commented, opening the door before I could alert her of my arrival.

"My bad. I ran into a hiccup, but I'm here." Offering no further explanation, I walked past Kross and went straight to her living room. Dropping my equipment on the floor, I removed my work jacket then headed to her kitchen.

"I'm not your girlfriend, Hollis. You don't have to lie to protect my feelings, ya know?"

Regardless, of her speech, her tone said differently. Tailing me through her home, I shook my head sensing Kross' eyes stuck to me as I washed my hands.

"I don't know who taught you that but lying is the opposite of what I'd do to protect your feelings, Kross. I ran into some bullshit and got sidetracked. I should've called. I'll say that much," I acknowledged, taking a chair from her dining table and walking it to the living room.

Wagging her finger, Kross issued a brooding stare. I wanted to smack her ass in the black sweats hugging her thighs or pinch one of her nipples in the loosely fitted graphic tee draped over her body, but she wasn't going for it.

"Stop being such pessimist," I counseled, covering her body with my barber's cape once I got her seated. The black smock swallowed her frame like I envisioned my arms would do. She didn't make a move or sound, just shut her eyes and produced a smile I could read.

We were quiet for the first five minutes of her cut. It took a lot not to groan and grip the soft curly hair on the top of her head that she threatened to kill me for cutting too short. Her home was quiet and warm. I didn't feel the need to speak until thoughts of Rock's warning ushered itself into my peace.

"Did you cut your hair when you went crazy or have you always worn it short?" I asked, seriously though it made us both laugh.

"No, foo'. I've always worn it this length."

"You remind me of Nia Long in the 'Best Man', your hair's just a little longer," I noted.

"Yeah, I've heard that before."

Finally working up the nerve, I asked Kross what I'd been wondering.

"Was the baby shower really the first time you've been out in years?"

"That was nearly two months ago and you're just now mentioning that? Is that what you heard?" she asked, her chin descending as the vibration of my clippers appeared to tickle the base of her neck. I didn't respond because she was right. Kross and I didn't speak every day but the few times we had since our chess game, I hardly brought up the way she lived.

"It's been a year, not years. And yes, my brother's event was the first time," she agreed, not appearing insecure about the reality.

"That's crazy. You don't seem extra cautious in the presence of strangers," I stammered, concentrating on the shape of her hairline and the length of her neck. Caressing the back of Kross collar, I asked that she relax.

"I wasn't amongst strangers; I was with family. And since my brother allowed you in the same room as me, you had to be worthy of my presence."

Chuckling, I thought of Kennedy and his own crazy antics at times. His credibility wasn't as solid as Kross made it out to be.

The outburst from the sports announcer giving their take on

today's game prompted Kross to lift her head and concentrate on the TV.

"Aww, that's bullshit! AB is just another T.O or Chad Johnson. All three have too much dip on they chip and ironically, they all play the same position," she demanded.

Shocked, I stood up straight. "Check you out sounding like you actually know what the hell you're talking about."

"Because I do," she scoffed, waving me off.

"As complex and untraditional as my household was when I was younger, sports and music were consistent. Just like Derek Carr's fuckups," she joked, flicking my Raiders' fitted from the table with her feet.

"Pretty toes and all, you better keep them dogs on the floor."

"Shut up! You know I'm know right," she challenged glancing over her shoulder like I was working on her head.

"At least my man's has ethics, unlike your boy Brady," I spat back.

"If that ain't the pot calling the kettle black? Did you forget you showed your ass during the baby shower games?"

Shrugging, I grinned recalling what she was referring to.

"Shit, you shouldn't play if you're not tryna win," I bellowed, proving her point. "Besides, I never claimed to be a team-player. I'm too selfish for that."

"Guess that's why we're both single and self-employed. Too selfish for direction," she murmured while I moved to her side.

"Head to the side," I directed.

"Be gentle," she shrieked.

"And remember, you asked me for a favor. Don't start insulting me," I whispered, focusing on the curl of her natural hair.

"Ha, there's another S-word that applies. Sensitive," she instigated, lightheartedly.

"I also love sex and sucking succulent titties," I notated since she wanted to be an asshole.

"You're nasty," she blushed, her bottom lip becoming locked between white teeth. "And let's be clear," she continued. "You're returning a favor. You're not just doing this out the kindness of your heart."

"You're right, I'm doing this because your edges were off deck, and I wanted to see you again. Like you said, selfish," I revealed, winking at her smitten behavior. "I'll also be stingy as hell, with you if you let me."

"Why do you want to?" she inquired, breathless now that I was directly in her face.

Muffled by my own unfamiliarity, my eyes got tight like hers. "I'm trying to figure that out but I don't think it's a bad thing."

Laughing awkwardly, Kross gently pushed me from her personal space.

"Are you almost done?" she asked, her raspy tone switching to lighter than a second ago.

"Almost. Don't interrupt perfection. What's with the crystals and stones. You got another order," I mentioned, pointing to a stash of multi-crystals scattered across her table.

"Yep. It seems the more I get back to the real world, the more my business is flourishing. Some days, I wish I could just have a cup of hot cocoa and listen to a good record but creating my own pieces is something I can't let go. It was the sole purpose of me being at *Body* in the first place, so I have to make it count," she said with a smile, obviously proud of what she'd done thus far.

"That's dope as hell. I'll have to cop something from your collection for Connor."

Clearing her throat like it were necessary, Kross asked what I knew she'd been thinking.

"Where's Connor's mom?"

I groused, aggravation tugging on my resolve prior to my reply. "In her fuckin' skin."

Cringing, Kross looked up at me. "That bad, huh?"

"It is, what it is. I got locked up at seventeen. Sadly being locked up was better than home at the time. I guess that's why I understand where you're coming from with your 'being away'," I acknowledged.

"Connor's mom, Ciara, was the first woman I'd met when I came home, and she was easy. I needed easy at the time, but now, she's vindictive. I would never want to take Connor away from her mother but I can't have her taint my daughter's impression of me or the world for that matter," I explained, cutting off my truth before it completely arose.

"Well, Connor seems like a brilliant little girl, who loves and respects her daddy. She will only think of you in the light you shine upon yourself. Trust me, I was raised by a pimp and no one could tell me my father wasn't a saint. People thought who he was outside of our home would tarnish the relationship I shared with my dad, it didn't," Kross posed.

Chuckling to myself, my brows wrinkled. "Oh, so we can talk about them now? Your family?"

"Ha! Ha! I mean you're letting me in, why not? And besides, we both know women don't play about their hair and considering I just let you cut mine, I think it's okay to open up a smudge," she recommended in the same sarcastic sneer I used.

"My daddy, Kenneth Karmer was wild in the streets and sometimes even brought the wrong lessons home but he was a good man. He was reliable, funny and genuine aside from what folks perceived from their lens. When I decided to work at his brothel, people didn't understand. I was initially hired as the accountant for *Body* but eventually, I started dabbling in other regards of the brothel when I decided to establish *Vibez* and needed more money. My parents didn't even know. I'm sure that's why it's still hard for my dad to accept how affected I was by the disaster; I wasn't supposed to be there in the first place," she shared, while I unhooked the cape from around her body. I probably should have been turned off by what she shared. The lady had just explained how her family business is affiliated with the sex industry, instead, I was entranced. Just like me, Kross had been through somethings that she couldn't run from and everyone around us was a constant reminder of it.

"What?" she asked tensely at my silence.

"You."

"Again, what?" she repeated.

"You're different, that's all. I get thrown off whenever reminded," I confessed, cutting my eyes in her direction.

Not thinking it through, I asked what I'd been wanting to since Connor snuck the phone under her bathroom sink. It had been almost three months since I started delivering packages to Kross personally and two since I'd laid eyes on her. I was done letting time pass when I knew where I wanted to be. The feeling was foreign yet refreshing.

"You wanna go out?"

"Not really," she replied truthfully. "Aside from the strides I've begun taking towards resurrection, I'm not firm on wanting to crack open that part of my vault," she further expounded.

"You think life is going to allow you to strategically get back on your shit? Fate doesn't work that way, neither do blessings. I told you that," I recapped her, putting up my equipment though Kross remained seated.

Straightening her posture, Kross kept attempting to get me on her wave; I didn't feel her on this one. It was okay for her to get back to work, get back to family, but not to love? Or at least something that felt good.

"Look, Hollis, you're cool. You make me laugh, you challenge my stubbornness, and I like having someone to talk to without judgment, but... the last man I entertained was more comfortable with my profession as a prostitute than my PTSD. I don't want to lose the elements of us that make me smile by getting too deep."

Completely bypassing her sermon, I shook my head still standing over the conflicted beauty.

"I didn't ask you all of that. I'd like to take you out, on a date. I'll ensure the place is quiet and void of a million people. I understand what you need, Kross. I only want to hear you say no if you frankly don't want to go out with me, not because you don't want to leave your home. Trust me, this box can't save you from anything that's meant for you. I'm just asking for your presence and considering I've already had it a few times you're being an ass by saying no."

Leaning into my personal space, Kross' aroma halted my coaching. It was as if her defense vanished, and her novelty premiered a white flag that quickly. Without a stammer, Kross pulled me down to her by my polyester polo and gave me her lips. Gripping the arms of the chair holding Kross, I relished in our tongues directing our intentions. Naturally, my left hand inched up to her face, feigning for the sensation of her pronounced cheeks against my palm. When Daisy's nosey ass started barking, common sense reintroduced itself.

"Wait! I'm sorry," Kross defended, completely out the chair and on her feet.

"For what?" I questioned, hating how harsh our detachment felt.

"I'm sorry for being forward and confusing. I freaking stuttered when you asked to take me on a date, then I turn around and suck your lips like we're old lovers. That's weird," she commented, scolding herself.

"Call it weird, call it you, it doesn't change what I asked of you. And if you didn't know, new lovers kiss as if they'll never see each other again too," I flirted, extending my index finger from the center of her chest up to her small nose.

"Check it. I'm not trying to force shit, but I don't feel like that's what I'm doing. I get you've been through a lot but you gotta enjoy the breeze and chill baby," I schooled. The earnestness was evident in my delivery. "I mean, we either go out or you cook."

"I thought we'd been through this. I don't cook but if you prepare the meal tonight i'll clean up the mess," she bargained, leaning against the chair I was only seconds from fucking her on.

"If you agree to a date, I'll cook and clean. I'll do it all, you just gotta let me," I confirmed, moving towards her kitchen as if she'd already given an answer.

Snickering, my new friend called out to me as I disappeared. "I guess I don't have much of a choice."

"You guessed right," I reinforced.

Through Kross didn't cook, she made sure to keep her fridge fully stocked. Before I could get the chicken cleaned and the potatoes cut, she ran into the kitchen while putting on a *Supreme* hoodie in a hurry.

"What's wrong?"

"Truth's having the baby!"

CHAPTER ten

KROSS

"Aye!"

"B," I shouted back, disgusted by the heightened lust that swept through my body at the sound of Hollis' dominance. He was an asshole and knew it. I kind of liked that he was an asshole and sadly, he knew that too.

The impatient giant had been downstairs waiting on me for nearly thirty minutes and his hastiness was clear. I was surprised, yet extremely thankful he hadn't wandered upstairs to get me.

Sitting on my bed, I snapped my rose gold *Vibez* anklet and fastened the straps of my black Prada heels. I didn't know where exactly we were going, but I hoped my black pants, and off the shoulder blouse were acceptable. Deliberately, I inhaled and exhaled preparing myself for the night and its possibilities. Honestly, I wasn't simple enough to trust that this night would be easy. Regardless of Hollis and I spending time alone, we were drifting into unveiling territory. We were shuffling into a space that may have this man looking at me buck-eyed and running for the heavens. My confidence was unstable and I didn't know if Hollis would remain a shield in the middle of chaos as he had been indoors.

Then what the hell are you doing going on a date with him? I thought aloud.

"Aye! You have a minute to come downstairs or I'm coming up to see what the hell is really taking you so long. Considering your hair is the length of a—"

"Watch it, Jay-Z nose. You wish I'd give you the pleasure of running, let alone sniffing this bobby pin length hair," I joked, narrowing my eyes as I came into view on the top of my stairs.

"Damn, you fine," Hollis professed, brushy brows slightly touching at his admitted gratitude. I grinned seeing hands I'd dreamt about slide in the pockets of his army green pants as if he was confused as to where to put them.

"Really? That's it? You don't have an insult to accompany that praise?"

Quietly, Hollis shook his head. I could tell he'd had the hair he usually wore wild, twisted while the sides were tapered. I couldn't hide the pleasure my senses felt catching whiffs of the pineapple oil coating his scalp. I also took note of the multi-colored button-down fitting Hollis' broad shoulders as if tailor-made.

"You don't look too bad yourself. Top of your head went from Lil Wayne to Ace Hood style" I countered, allowing my fingers to freely entertain his sharpened hairline.

When Hollis opened my front door and moved aside for me to exit, I was curbed.

"If you stopped pushing yourself, you'll stop growing, beautiful."

Latching my hand around his, I allowed Hollis to guide me down my porch and to his all-black Mercedes Benz. I grinned, thinking of all this man had shared with me. It had taken him years to get his life moving in a direction he was happy with. I was happy to ride shotgun with him.

"You really do look beautiful, Kross."

"I'm not underdressed, am I? You know I'm not big on the dressy stuff," I acknowledged, pulling the sun visor down for the second time since getting in the car.

Cutting off my reflection of myself, Hollis reached over and closed the overhead view.

"Stop doing that. Overthinking. You're perfect."

"Far from it," I shot back.

"Depends on your definition."

"I'm far from perfect. I've done some crooked shit that eliminated that word from any description of me a long time ago. Now, Connor, she's perfect," I stated, hoping the conversation would steer and meaning what I'd said.

"Ha! That little demon is a different kind of perfect. She makes me proud to be alive, just to see her grow up. She hasn't forgotten about that promise you made either."

"Oh, I know. She's texted me twice since I agreed to come to see her performance. She serious about playing the guitar too," I countered, noticing we were already pulling into the restaurant. I thought it was cute we were having dinner at a Mexican restaurant since I mentioned how much I love the cuisine more than once, and ironically, Hollis shared my love.

"You should teach her. I don't mind paying you," he finally responded, handing the valet his keys and taking my hand as I slid out the leather seat.

"Your pockets aren't heavy enough," I teased, pinching his cheek.

Hardly through the entrance, I took note of the sort of crowded place.

"There's a lot of people here," I whispered, trying not to be reckless with my complaints. Without thinking, my body was tucked behind Hollis' as he spoke to the hostess.

"Yeah, that's how restaurants with good food on the menu work," he suggested, looking down at me with a crooked smirk.

"You're so funny," I chimed.

"You're fine, Kross. You're always fine with me," he comforted me, squeezing my fingers between his as we were led to a table near the kitchen. Pulling away, I frowned with panic tugging at my eyes.

"Where's the exit? I know we requested a seat near the exit," I fussed, my aggravation no longer disguised as we took a seat. Hollis ordered drinks for both of us since I obviously needed a second to get myself together. Once the waitress disappeared, Hollis went off.

"Kross, look at me," Hollis damn near yelled when my eyes danced around the wide space plotting my escape route.

"You said you were ready for this, Kross."

"I thought I was," I barked. For a person who had been pretty much caged for a year, a temperamental asshole serving as a chaperone wasn't ideal.

"If you want to leave, we can. I don't want you uncomfortable," Hollis reasoned, pulling my attention to his protection.

"Though I could snatch off your legs for believing I'd allow anything to happen to you, I can admit that I don't have to understand your feelings to respect them."

Shutting my eyes briefly, I released my lids and recognized I wasn't the only one examining our surroundings closely.

"Expecting someone?" I questioned.

Quickly, Hollis' mahogany orbs found me. "No."

"Then why are you watching everyone here suddenly except for me? Do not make me wonder about you. I still haven't figured out how *we* got *here*," I confessed, becoming more and more unsettled by the moment.

"Call it fate," he beamed, sipping from the lemon water our server brought over.

"Bullshit. There's no such thing as fate," I grunted, checking the menu.

Reaching across the table, Hollis' fingers found my chin. "Then call it a blessing."

"For who," I whispered, abandoning my frustration in his flirting.

"Hell, both of us. God doesn't make mistakes and regardless of what you say because you're uneasy, it doesn't change the fact that you like me and there's a connection between us. You have a problem with it? Take it up with the big man."

Unable to conjure a decent response, I said the first thing that came to mind.

"Shut up!" I was unable to control the giggle that followed.

"Make me," he countered, causing me to modify my body in the leather seat beneath me. Aside from anything I'd experienced over a year, I was still a woman and a fine ass man made my pussy flex just like the next. My interest being intact without any financial exchange was more surprising to me than anything. I couldn't dissect if it was substance arising in my mortality or stupidity steering my seclusion as my daddy would suggest.

"I guess big nose is pretty impressionable," he added, elevating the warm tension wrapping around us.

"Or maybe that pretty little girl you make work the day shift is pretty clever. Wonder where she gets her scheming ways from," I joked, thinking of the wicked things my dad was responsible for teaching me.

"Connor gets her intelligence and everything else good about her from the same place. Me," he answered proudly.

Without thinking, I blurted a question I was dying to know. "You want more kids?"

"With you?" he interrogated. I wanted so badly to say, yes but knew there was a chance he was just being sweet.

Dropping my head, my fingers found my ear. "Stop playing. I'm being serious."

"So am I," he replied firmly, this time reaching over and removing my digits from their solace.

"I'm speaking in general. You know what, let's just drop it."

"Don't get upset because the subject isn't easy. I'm not rushing you to say how you feel. Would you like to have children of your own one day?"

Grateful for the mature approach he'd alternated to, I decided to match his energy.

"Truthfully, it's not something I really considered before. Though I've been writing for the paper for years, I thought I'd be running *Body* one day. Unlike my parents, I didn't want to raise a child in *that* life. Being brought up with the notion that a man can touch if he could pay or being raised to call the women who also sleep with my father, auntie, I didn't want that for my babies Frankly, I would have needed a man who was okay with my lifestyle and most weren't. Plus, I don't think I'm the mothering type."

Hollis laughed. "The way you take care of Daisy makes me think different. And I noticed you answered the question with the terms of your old life being the anchor. You're not still working in a brothel; you aren't still being trained to become a madam. I'm asking the woman who's sitting across from me now. The woman who's taking a chance on me, her business and heart again," Hollis responded.

"Well, in that case," I admitted. "I'd love to have a house full of kids and to experience family in a traditional sense. House, dog, kids, husband, all that."

"Tradition has never been my strong point, but you make it sound like an enticing task," the handsome man flirted.

"Don't try to gas me, Hollis. I know three kids, a home in this economy, and a healthy marriage to a man who isn't fond of the system in the first place is damn near impossible. I bet your mom loses her mind having such a loose son. I guess that's better than it being Holly, I joked, trying to bring up two people he rarely mentioned, but swore was all he had.

Hollis had me so distracted with openness; I'd forgotten how uncomfortable I was ten minutes before and I wanted the same transparency.

"My mom stopped being concerned with me a long time again. And anything's possible, Ms. Peach Street. Hell, I got you to come out the house," Hollis answered as if he had a direct link to the thoughts drifting around in my head.

Staring at the roof of the restaurant, I spoke slowly. "True but let's be real, you didn't set this up alone. Had it been all your doing, we'd still be screaming at one another through my intercom. We've spent enough time together at this part to know and admit neither of *us* usually does *this*."

Cockily, a broad grin slithered over the chocolate man's face as he reached for his drink.

"I don't entertain shit I don't want to; I don't give a damn who orchestrates it. You aren't the only person with a closet full of shit that keeps you hidden in other rooms in your world. I told you that before. So, although Connor got you on the phone, I was already plotting on coming back to your doorstep."

"Well, excuse me for not placing the credit appropriately. You seem like a man that thrives off notary," I teased, fluffing the longer parts of my hair.

"Nah, I'm not that egotistical. But what you see, is what you get and I don't go out of my way to give more than what I have. That strain can be detrimental," Hollis confessed, refusing to reconnect his eyes after his admission.

"Good because I'm not big on expectations. My parents drilled in my head actions versus the gamble a long time ago."

"Going about shit that way may be the cause of you losing out on some beautiful possibilities," Hollis hinted, his eyes tapering as I gave him a peek into my reservations.

Cleaning residue of complimentary chips and salsa from the corners of my mouth, I nodded in agreeance though I wasn't one hundred percent in alignment with Hollis' statement.

"I unlatched myself from expectations when I realized nothing but personal conviction could lead a person. Be it to love, violence, hell, everything; it's all a personal choice. Even with outside influences, we hold the power and we do a shitty job with our control. Unfortunately, even before the shooting and fire I realized my kindness wasn't a contingency for folks to do right by me, so I said fuck em'. That's why it's been so easy for me to stay away for a year. Trust me, Hollis, I've been gone a lot longer."

"And sadly, you didn't have the right muthafuckas looking for you," he replied menacingly.

Right on time, our waitress trespassed on our space. I was taken aback when the redhead placed fresh cocktails directly in front of myself and my date.

"I didn't order this," I informed her, already pushing the glass back towards her serving tray.

Confused, the young server peeked in the direction of another table. "Umm, I was told to bring them over," she stuttered.

"Did you not hear what she said?" Hollis interrupted, pushing from the table slightly.

"Hollis," I muttered, prompting his glare to come back to me and his anger to lessen.

"Look, sir. I don't mean any disrespect. The gentlemen near the door asked that I bring over the drinks and let you know, you won," she blurted, grinning shyly and peering between our table and the one holding three gentlemen who I'd never seen.

"Take that shit back to the bar," Hollis growled, his stature shrinking in the seat across from me.

Shuffling her weight between antsy legs, the young woman shook her head. "I can't take the drinks back; it'll be my third return for the night. They'll think I'm doing something wrong. I just got this job," she trembled.

"You have nothing to apologize for. Did that table of animals say what exactly Mr. Hollis won?" I meddled already having an idea and praying I was wrong. This mess was too cliché to actually be true. The tickled expressions on their faces further validated my assumptions. Adding to the disaster, one of the men left his seat and joined us in the cut.

"Well, it looks like you got me. I'm a man of my word so first thang in the morning, I'll have your bread," the new face rambled like it was decent to confess in my presence.

Since the younger Danny DeVito was dead set on sharing, I probed. "What exactly did he win?"

Drunkenly, he chuckled. "You, Ms. Peach Street."

"Wow," was all I could manage to say.

Nodding somberly, I looked to a silent Hollis who, unfortunately, sat across from me with his best poker face on.

"I should've known this was too good to be true. Fuck you, Hollis," I managed to say in between my suddenly dry mouth and sick disposition. Jumping up, I got three steps away before Hollis was on my heels.

"Kross! Kross, please wait. Can we talk about this? Leaving would be you being immature," he had to nerve to shout.

"You bet on me, Hollis! Is that not fucking immature enough for you? You and your dickhead friends don't know the half of what I've been through and you bet your minimum wage salaries on me. Those pennies couldn't buy my time, let alone my pussy!" I barked, totally forgetting where I was and no longer caring who was privy to what was going on.

Invading the distance, I'd placed between us, Hollis came closer.

"Check it out, I know you're pissed but watch your mouth. I'm not disrespecting you, Kross," he growled.

Laughing menacingly, I shook my head. "You already have, Hollis."

Pushing him back, I ignored the look of sadness hovering over his face and the mumbles coming from onlookers. As I made it to the exit, I cursed myself once I'd realized I'd forgotten my personal belongings.

"Kross, listen to me," Hollis started once I reappeared passing the table of assholes who were snickering minutes ago. Holding my elbow, Hollis guided my body in his direction. I'm sure we looked like idiots discussing this in a room full of people.

"Just give me a second to explain then I'll take you home. I know you're pissed but you'll get home how you got here. What we did was some childish bullshit. You were isolated and we were curious. The bet was never about getting to know you or smashing. Just getting to see you."

Holding back an emotion I hated to be so accustomed to, I grinned. "Well, do you see me now? Am I as broken as you all thought?" I spat.

Out of nowhere, the sound of shattering glass, and yelling clogged my concentration. Following my instincts, I sheepishly crawled under the first table in sight.

"What the fuck?" I heard one of the men dressed in a uniform

I'd seen countless times, screech. My hands covered my ears, failing at blocking out the noise that didn't resemble the comfort of my heartbeat. A heartbeat that reminded me that I was still breathing. I didn't care about being embarrassed or tasteful, I wanted to feel safe.

"Kross," I heard a deep voice called out. I didn't respond, just covered my ears and rocked my body. The coldness of the restaurant's floor coating my bare ankles was a strange relief.

"Ms. Peach Street," Hollis called out, this time triggering my eyes to shift. I watched him lower on his knees beside me.

"It was just glass. You're fine, my love," he attempted to assure me.

Slowly removing my hands, I steadied my shaking. "It was just glass," I chanted.

"You're fine, Kross."

Again, I repeated his words. "I'm fine?"

Nodding, Hollis reached his hand out to me. When I didn't counter his gesture, he rose on his knees to look over the table.

"Get the hell up. You see her down there," Hollis ordered. I didn't hear one objection as all the men abandoned their seats on my behalf.

Rejoining me, Hollis grinned.

"This isn't what I imagined when thinking of you being on your knees," he blurted as if it was okay.

"Not funny."

"I just know I fucked up and don't know what to say or how to fix it," he admitted.

Taking in a few breaths, I snarled at Hollis.

"There's nothing to say. Just take me home and go collect your chump change, champ."

CHAPTER Eleven

HOLLIS

Today was the first time in a while that I was forced to be the boss when I didn't have the desire. It took every ounce of my work ethic to slide out of bed and not spend another day wondering how the stunt I pulled could have set Kross back. I had never considered myself a huge empathic but the panicked expression on her disappointed face had been haunting me for days.

"Man, you're crazy. I would've pocketed that stack with no problem. You going soft on us, Hollis?" Josh baited playfully.

"Shut the hell up! You niggas are tacky pulling that shit at the restaurant. Broke ass didn't even have the money on you," I yelled, shoulder bumping an amused Moses. I wondered if I drenched his Prostyle head in water, would shit still be so comical. Kross was hurt in the midst of our bullshit and wasn't shit amusing about that. And sadly, I didn't consider that until the damage was done.

"You won fair and square, boss man. How were we to know you had fucked around and fell for the cat lady?"

I cut my eyes. "Watch your fucking mouth."

"She's beautiful by the way. I can see how you lost track of your mission. She reminds me of a young Nia Long," he further explained. I didn't give a damn about his compliment, I'd much rather he'd kept it to himself.

Smacking my teeth, I grilled Moses through a hot temper.

"Man, get on. You knew what the hell you were doing. If I didn't think you'd act like a little bitch, I'd fired your ass. That shit was out of line and you know it."

"Aww, come on boss man! Why are you upset with me? You won!"

"I didn't win shit, I lost. She won't even take my calls," I confessed, knowing the change in my tone was obvious. I didn't give a damn. I never cared about anyone's perception of who I dealt with; I wasn't going to start now.

Giving his perspective, Rocky cut in. "I bet she won't talk to you. Your ass put a price on her."

"Rock, I get it, but damn, I'm trying," I said almost sounding like Connor when she thought I'd let her give up on something I knew she wanted.

"You trying by doing what? Apologizing? Nigga you supposed to do that. You fucked up and didn't tell her before someone else could. An apology is the least you could offer. I don't know Kross, but I can tell you gon' have to ante up to fix this one, kid."

Before I could respond, Kennedy stomped through the door and over to me. His hands gripping the collar of my uniform shirt, put my emotions back on ten. The others attempted to break us up but not before we'd started swinging. Like Guerillas in a confined box, we thumped and swung completely ruining the lunchroom I'd taken pride in setting up.

"Come on man, you niggas are tripping," Rock yelled, pulling me away while others went to Kennedy.

"Boy, have you lost your fucking mind?" I screamed, deep breathes rushing through my nostrils like a fucking bull. This was just the pain reliever I needed.

"Didn't I ask you to leave my sister alone? Told you she wasn't your type of woman and you just had to cross the line," Kennedy yelled; Rocky and the other guys looking on in confusion but were mindful to keep us separate. Other than my feelings for Kross, I'd failed to tell them that Kennedy was her brother.

"What the hell is going on?" Rock asked, his body positioned in front of me. Pushing him back, my blood was boiling.

"Aye check it out. I'm going to give you a minute because I know you're pissed about your sister and I go to war for mine. But I'm going to need you to remember even quicker who the hell I am."

Reneging, Kennedy released his grip, adding a hard push to his movement.

"Didn't I ask that you leave my sister alone? I knew you'd break her heart and out of respect, I asked you to back up. You just said fuck me huh, Hollis?"

Stepping forward, Moses spoke at the wrong time as always.

"Man, I know you're pissed but it was just a joke. This can't be as serious as y'all are making it."

Meshing the shorter man, Kennedy invaded Moses' breathing room when he resumed his balance. "Nigga, my sister's feelings aren't a fucking game."

"Neither is my feelings *for* your sister. I care about Kross," I voiced, straightened my clothes out. At this instance, I knew my feelings for Kross were real. Anybody else would've been invited to the parking lot to get more aggression out. However, I didn't beat Kennedy's ass like I could've because I knew it would bring Kross more strife.

Snarling, the angry older brother snatched away from Josh, who figured the struggle between us wasn't over.

"That's not how it came back to me."

"I don't give a shit how you heard it. Kross is pissed and I understand that. But I'm telling you from my mouth, I care about that woman and I don't need anybody to press me about how I made her feel. I feel it, nigga," I spat, bumping his shoulders as I exited the lunchroom. If I stayed any longer, there was no guaranteed we'd be able to keep our hands to ourselves.

Already on my way to pick up Connor, I groaned forgetting to call my sister beforehand.

"Yes, Hollis," Holly answered in a chipper mood. I was grateful my sister had climbed out of her own funk after dealing with a fool who couldn't keep his hands to himself. And like I said, I went hard for my sister so I sympathized with Kennedy.

"Ma there?"

Sighing, Holly replied more evenly. "No."

"Good. I'll be there in like fifteen."

After a pause, I knew Holly recognized my mood.

"You good?"

Being honest, I told Holly I'd explained everything once I got to our mother's house. My sister and I always had a tight relationship, yet the same couldn't be said for our mother and me.

Our relationship was complicated. She held a lot of resentment in her heart after my choices costed her more than she'd worked for. I wanted to believe it was just the money she'd lost on my account that tainted our relationship but I'd paid her back years ago, and still, she gave me the minimum.

Walking into the open door, I grew annoyed when I didn't see Connor's in sight. She'd gotten out of school hours ago and considering it was Thursday, she didn't have play rehearsal.

"Hey, Holly. Where's Connor? Don't tell me she went with your mama. I'm ready to go home and crash, man," I complained, knowing I sounded way more emotional than usual.

"First off, your attitude is ugly. Secondly, yes, Connor went with her grandmother to the store. They should be on their way back by now."

Sitting on the couch across from her, I didn't respond.

"You can't just pick your kid up and leave. Ma would actually like to see you sometimes. and not just during drop-offs."

"Man, if Connor being here after school is a problem, I can make other arrangements," I defended, knowing Holly wasn't saying what I was implying.

Raising a finger, my big sister shut me down. "Don't do that. You know damn well, I have no problem looking after my niece when you're working. I'm telling you, we don't feel the love, asshole."

Shaking my head, my brows dipped at her criticism. "Are you serious? Don't I make sure everybody straight? Nobody wants for anything."

"You think that takes place of your presence, Hollis?"

"I don't know, let's ask Edison if we can pay the bill with affection," I replied, mockingly.

Throwing a pillow at me, Holly narrowed her round eyes. "What's the deal with you? You're being more of a jerk today than usual."

Second-guessing my thoughts on sharing, I relaxed my head against the couch cushion instead of answering.

Giggling, Holly blurted what she'd already known.

"I don't know why you frontin', I already heard you're in the doghouse?"

"And let me guess, you heard that from your nosy ass niece. She tells you way too much of what's going on in my life," I stated, reaching for the remote.

"Don't do Connor like that. She worships the ground you walk on and has good intentions. It's not her fault life happens and she has something to say about it," Holly defended. If you asked her, Connor could do no wrong.

"Yeah, well, she should be talking to me about her feelings."

"Really? Get the hell outta here acting like you weren't the same kid that would rather sleep outside than in the house because you felt ma didn't understand you? Judgment isn't cute on you, bruh."

Smiling, I recalled the incident my sister was referring to.

"Listen, if you need to talk, I'm here. I know you've been assuming the role of the eldest sibling as of lately but that doesn't mean I can't return the love in ways outside of financial. Tell me what's going on with you and this lady you like," she advised, making the counseling session too enticing to pass on.

For almost a year, I'd been taking on some of my family's financial responsibilities. The nigga my sister fell in love with caused her to have to start over and my mom just always had a hard time catching up once she'd fallen behind on bills. Unluckily, her time at bingo didn't help the situation. As the only man in their lives, I made sure they were straight even when I wasn't around. I appreciated Holly trying to return the love.

Sighing deeply, I shared with my sister what was on my heart.

"I fucked up Holly and I don't know if I can fix it. Crazy thing is, I actually want to," I said, messing with my hair.

"I told you a little about Kross, but the real reason I started speaking to her in the first place was because of a bet I made with Moses."

"Your driver?" she squealed, slapping me upside my head.

Peering over at her heavy-handed ass, I grunted. "Man, what the hell!"

"Ugh, cut the damn whining, I barely touched you. You know you're wrong. I thought you said Kross suffers from PTSD and you still—"

"I know. I know. I messed up. Her brother works for Brown Brothas and is actually a good friend of mine and he flexed when he saw me earlier today. All that tells me is she's talking about it and her thoughts of me don't include any of what made her give me a chance in the first place," I stated.

"Yeah, because she's second-guessing herself. She doesn't want to think of good times because then she'll be fishing for the signs she missed of your disloyalty in a memory. How fair is that?" Holly questioned.

"I don't doubt any of that. You know, normally I don't play too much into emotions unless it's my kid's, but I can't shake the guilt. I could've beat Moses' ass for laying the scheme out in front of her."

"Oh, instead of keeping it going behind her back like you?"

"You know what I mean, Holly. I really like Kross, I would've told her eventually. After the wedding and babies at least," I recognized, knowing it was wrong.

"Wow, I've never heard you mention marriage without it including the name of one of your hoes or without your face balled up like something close by stinks," my sister teased, mocking an expression I guess was a replica of my disdain for the sentiment.

"Yeah, well, shit changes," I shrugged.

Bringing the conversation back to its focal, Holly pressed me for a resolution.

"What are you going to do to fix this? I can tell from this conversation and the way Connor speaks of this woman, she's something special."

"I don't know if there's anything I can do. She's blocked my number already and refuses to answer the door when I stop by. Even her dog don' turned on me."

"And what else are you going to do? If your apology is this short-lived maybe you should leave her be."

Cutting my eyes, I grimaced. "Don't measure my feeling, Holly. I never said I was giving up, just said I hadn't figured out what to do from this point."

"If you're serious and you know Kross doesn't want to see or talk to you, make her feel your presence even without seeing your face."

"Man, I'm not stalking that girl," I blurted prematurely.

"No foo! As someone who experienced domestic violence, why the hell would I propose that?"

"My bad."

"Try to show her that your time wasn't in vain and regardless of initial intent, you care. What's something she revealed to love that you know will put a smile on her face without putting her in the position to have to deal with you when she's not ready? You can't force her to be where you are but you can meet her halfway."

Quietly, I thought it over. Holly was right, I had to compromise and not go pushing myself on a woman who didn't trust me.

"I get what you're saying, sis. I'll put some thought into it."

"I know he's here, I saw his car outside," I heard Connor say while entering the house.

Getting up to meet her at the door, I gave my sister some love.

"Imma head out. I'll let you know how things go," I assured

her, thankful to have some direction when it came to guiding Kross back to the place of security we'd conquered.

Clearing her throat, Holly's mumbles prompted me to peer at her before grabbing Connor.

"You know you're going to have to talk to mom eventually, right?"

"Yeah, well, eventually ain't today."

CHAPTER Twelve

Kross

I knew surrendering was a mistake.

I knew even being outside the lines of perfection, Hollis was a gamble I may not have been able to afford.

I knew he would ruffle my focus on survival but still, I relinquished my doubt and now I'm pulling myself out of humiliation, again.

"Tell me what's on your mind, Kross. I can see the wheels going crazy in your head. What do you feel?"

"Played. I feel like no matter what, my feelings will continue to be either taken advantage of or treated like a joke. Hollis seemed like he was above either sentiment."

"And now?"

"And now, I don't know what to think. I had this ridiculous thought that because he knew my brother that would play a part in the way he treated me. Again, I put someone else in the position to protect me instead of ensuring that much myself."

Smiling, Dr. Sway nodded. "You said you don't know how you feel but it sounds to me you know exactly what you feel. And now I ask, outside of the deception or mannishly gesture Hollis displayed, do you think the same manipulation went for the connection you two share? We both know no one is perfect and everyone makes mistakes. Is Hollis' discretion bigger than a second chance or are you ready to forgive and move on separately?"

"It's only been two weeks," I grunted.

"Who said there's a time restraint on forgiveness. You're not required to hold on to grief for a set amount of time, Kross. However, I would advise that you forgive yourself for being vulnerable prior to giving that consideration to Hollis."

Crossing my legs, I concentrated on the sway of my Fila shoelaces. "I'm not there yet."

It had been weeks and I was still in a tug-of-war on how to proceed. Truth, Kennedy and Dr. Sway all tried to guide me in some direction and sadly the only person who could navigate my emotions, I didn't trust. I wanted to stay buried under disappointed that required little from me other than simply being still, but that wasn't an option. After almost losing your life, a subtle dose of heartache was like endearing a tongue bite; it wasn't the worst but still hurt like hell. I felt like a fucking fool standing in the center of a restaurant hearing that the man I thought was safe, wasn't.

The ringing of Dr. Sway's alarm clock concluded our session for the day. Rattling off my assignment for the week, I left the office still as conflicted as when I walked in.

Arriving home just as the sunset, I fed Daisy before pulling out my guitar for a session. The feeling of my fingers fleeting over the strings served as a release every time. Creating a sound that embodied my feelings was power to me. It stimulated elements of my confidence and reminded me of my control. No one could ever take that away from me.

Annoyed by my vibrating phone, I snatched it from the coffee table. When I saw Connor's number, I answered cautiously. Hollis had been trying to speak to me without pause, stooping so low as to take Connor's phone to communicate wasn't outlandishly.

"Hello?"

"Kross? I know you may not want to talk to me since my dad

screwed up but my mom didn't answer the phone and neither did my auntie Holly," she explained.

"I told you before, what's going on with your dad and I has nothing to do with you. As long as he's okay with it, I don't mind you calling. Now, what's wrong, Connor?" I wanted to know, moving my guitar out of the way. I smiled seeing her interest again piqued by the wooden item.

"Well, there's this boy... in my class and he... likes to pick on me," Connor stuttered. She'd barely gotten the concern out before I was on it.

"Who the hell is— wait. Messing with you how?" When Connor turned, I could see she was in her bedroom. I didn't want to be concerned, hell, it was none of my business but I wanted to ask so badly, where her dad was. I knew how he was about Connor having too much privacy, so if her door was closed, he was on his way in.

"His name is Phillip, and he's my age. One time, he walked by my desk and purposely knocked my things off. I ended up getting in trouble since I tripped him on his way back to his seat, it was totally unfair. And yesterday, I was studying my lines for the recital, and he comes over with his stupid friends and pours water all on my papers!"

I grimaced; lip hiked up with all the hostility I knew Connor felt. "Oh, hell nah!"

"Exactly," she agreed, matching my tone. "Sorry," Connor offered timidly at the pensive look I gave.

"I'm just so mad! I would say what Brandon's doing is bullying but then today, one of his friends told me that he actually likes me and that's the reason he's always picking with me. That's what I need help understanding; it doesn't sound right to me"

Grinning, I started to comprehend what Connor was experiencing. She was a beautiful little girl and smart as a whistle, there was no doubt little Brandon had a crush.

"Well, believe it or not, some people don't know how to properly convey their feelings. Their approach may be too aggressive, too nonchalant or just all wrong. It's not your job to sort through that little knucklehead's approach, you're the prize. The key is managing how you respond. He'll keep picking at you if he sees it gets under your skin. Sit on your throne and only come down when he's figured out how to properly get your attention," I instructed, winking when her eyes calmed at my explanation.

"Yeah, you're right. I'll just ignore him until he comes correct," she boasted.

"Who the hell is *him*?" A deep voice barreled through the room she rested inside and over the line. I couldn't even see his face and my hands were already shaking. His voice carried and his presence was thick enough to choke a bear.

"Connor, I'll talk to you later, okay? Let me know how it goes later in the week," I told her, attempting to get off the line without having to hang up on her.

Jumping on her bed, Hollis looked like shit when entering the frame. It hadn't been *that* long and I hadn't learned all his confronts but I knew the tension tight eyes, unenthused lips and black beanie so low it looked like he wanted to cover his face, wasn't Hollis' best look. He looked exactly how I felt, defeated. That brought little relief to my core considering I really liked Hollis, I wasn't okay with people I cared for being upset.

"I miss you," he acknowledged, staring so intensively, I could feel the heat blaring through the camera. I don't even know for certain that he blinked. At the moment, I refused to let him know that it mattered.

"Kross—"

"Connor, remember what I said."

Groaning, Hollis stood with her phone in his possession. Walking outside of range, Hollis spoke between scrunched teeth.

"Kross, baby, you have to listen to me."

"No! When you should've been talking, you weren't. Fuck off, Hollis," I yelled, getting pissed as he told me what I *had* to do versus asking. I knew that was just his nature but I didn't have compassion for his rituals and I deserved for Hollis to move outside the lines of *his* normalcy.

"You're right. This is all on me and I get it but how am I supposed to fix this if you don't let me?"

Shrugging, I twisted my lips. "I don't know. I mean, you figured out how to get to me when I wouldn't let you. I'm sure it's not impossible to figure out what to do next. Doing nothing at all is also an option." And with that, I disconnected the call before he could push. As much as I missed Hollis, seeing his face was enough to conclude I wasn't ready to patch things up. I'd gone from hurt to angry. I couldn't look at him without grimacing or having a thought of deceit bubbling over at my disposal. Nevertheless, I wasn't one-hundred percent sure Hollis wasn't worthy of a second chance. Outside of the big reveal, I'd accused him of being too honest at times, though it was appreciated.

Screaming into a throw pillow, I sneered seeing the frightened look on Daisy's face. "Don't act like I don't have to endure you're howling more times than not."

With my mind moving swiftly, I decided to shut down my session, shower and go to bed.

The next morning, I set sealing the packaging on the order I'd received. I still didn't know much about the client. Other than a few emails exchanged about the order status, there'd been no communication. Most of my customers allowed me to create in solace, however, not many spent thousands of bucks for their pieces, so I was a bit more curious. After what Hollis did, I deserved to be a bit pushy.

With the "F*ckboy" playlist I created for my readers and my damn self, blaring throughout my home, I frowned hearing someone ring my doorbell. Shocked, I went over and checked the camera.

"Yes," I answered, pressing the button for the intercom.

"Good morning. I have a delivery for a Ms. Peach Street," the man, dressed in a Brown Brothas' uniform announced.

I grew furious recognizing the round man's face from the night at the restaurant.

"Get the hell off my doorstep. I'm not going to continue to play games with a group of grown-ass men."

Exhaling impatiently, he paced back and forth while shaking his head. I was giving him ten seconds before sending Daisy outdoors.

"This isn't a game. The package is for you. It requires a signature but I'll just leave it here."

"Hollis wouldn't like that," I blurted.

Smirking, the impatient man waved off the notion. "He'll be alright, I'm sure. Enjoy your morning, ma'am."

I waited until the sketchy man was out the gate, and off my street before opening the door and retrieving what he'd left. One box had a 'hot' label on it and a little handle to hold, while the other was flat, wide and square. Opening the smaller of the two, I grinned seeing a fresh cup of Braulio Brew hot cocoa sitting inside. If I needed any confirmation that the contents were courtesy of Hollis Brown, I'd just received it. He was the only person I'd told about my love for the naturally made hot drink and after my advice to Connor; I knew Hollis had taken heed.

Rushing to my kitchen, I cut open the second package. Not having the paper completely removed, tears welled in my eyes sighting Prince's "Purple Rain" vinyl record I'd told Hollis I wanted when we first met. Quickly, I went back to the living room to play one of my favorite songs.

My fresh cocoa in one hand and the freedom of a new day pacing through the other, I two-stepped and sang the lyrics as if I wrote them. Another two repeats of the record and my mind settled on Hollis' move. Knowing he wasn't the most sentimental, I shut my eyes unable to steady my reaction. A cup of cocoa and a record wasn't worth my humiliation but neither was pretending I didn't want to be where Hollis was when I knew it was more uncomfortable being apart.

Chapter Thirteen

Hollis

"Hey, daddy. You look fly!" Connor approved, grinning from ear to ear. Nodding, I agreed.

"Well, I had a good stylist."

I had to admit it myself, she did a good job picking out my fit for the night. A black turtleneck, brown Corduroys was her choice and a good one. When we couldn't compromise on the shoes, I went with black Versace loafers and threw on a gold Franco chain for more of a vibe. Connor had to FaceTime me to see her work but she appeared happy all the same.

"Just think of what we talked about. Be a gentleman and remember you were in the wrong," Connor coached. I knew she was hoping things with Kross and I went well tonight, though our distance did little to affect their budding relationship. I was grateful that while Kross and I were on the outs, she still accepted Connor's calls. All her sincerity did was pull me back to our growing solace. It had been three weeks since shit hit the fan, and only days since Kross agreed to another date. I couldn't remember the last time I'd sought out a woman's companionship and Kross' rejection was just about enough for me to leave her alone as she'd requested. I went an entire day without sending a message that I knew she wouldn't answer but I couldn't stop thinking about her. Very little held my attention long enough for guilt and my hunger for Kross to disappear, so I stopped giving a fuck about my pride and put hers first. I'd disrespected a good woman by treating her pain like a gimmick, childishly putting a price on her sanity. That had never been me. I'd been on *that* side of the struggle and no matter how solid a person is, nobody wants to be the butt of a joke.

–"I gotcha, Connor. Just be sure to listen to your auntie and granny and don't have her driving you around all night looking for fucking Pokémon," I cautioned. Her awkward expression told me she'd already arranged a trip.

"Hey, as long as I give Auntie gas money, I don't see the problem." Just like me, Connor would go as far as a person would let her. If boundaries weren't set, she felt free to roam.

"Aye, I gotta go. I think Kross just pulled up. I'll send you a picture of the backyard in a minute," I promised.

Smacking her teeth, only because I couldn't thump her in the lip for doing so, Connor pouted.

"Please don't forget. After helping you hang thousands of lights and almost breaking my neck, I should at least be able to get a picture."

"Bye Connor," I voiced, rushing her off the phone. When my phone rang again, I groaned seeing the block number. I knew it was Shelby still trying her luck. In a minute, I was going to set up a meeting with Henry to request that he put his pup on a leash.

Catching a glimpse of Kross stepping from her car then anxiously checking the streets pushed me down my stairs quickly. I opened the front door right as the beauty's steps ceased at the end of my driveway.

"My bad. I should've been out here waiting on you," I greeted, witnessing her exhale deeply a few times.

Shaking her head, Kross averted eye contact. "It's okay, Hollis. I'm not that fragile. I can make it from here to the door," she retorted, sprawling a sarcastic tenor I'd grown to anticipate and adore coming from her. Lingering side by side as if the concrete beneath us had wheels, we held back. Fingers slightly brushing, sketchy breathes matching her impression of me was our bolster. I wanted to tell her how pretty she looked or how much our time apart showed me, I didn't like to be apart, yet, we stood still. Wading until she was ready to move, I resented the disconnect. Latching my fingers around hers, I brought Kross' hand up to my lips. The smell of chocolate mint spilled from her skin.

"Thank you for coming."

Nodding, she finally looked at me. "Can we go inside?" she tested, abruptly taking a step forward.

Following her lead, I told Kross about the set up in my backyard that I hoped she'd appreciate.

"Then lead the way," she pushed, slowing her stride. And with that I stepped in front of the patient woman, hands still entangled and guided her to our space for the night. Hardly through the side door of my home and the candles, roses and everything else that conjured light outdoors, was already igniting Kross' happy face.

"This all for me?" she investigated shocked, though there wasn't any need for her diffident. I fucked up, Kross wasn't the one who needed to be cautious. I deserved the doubt, not her. She looked gorgeous dressed in a leather overall dress, a turtleneck like mine and gold heels. Her growing hair was slicked back like a sexy businesswoman and her coating sparkled against the layers of lights that took hours to hang.

"This is really stunning, Hollis. I can't believe your mean self, did all of this. And truthfully, it has always been about an economic objective versus emotional in my life when it comes to apologizing, so I'm grateful for your actions," she whispered, speaking more words that fast than she'd said since arriving.

"I'm happy you like it. It was the least I could do. I can't front, Connor helped. A lot," I admitted, my hand going to the top of her ass as I directed her further into my yard. I smirked at the shiver I felt pass through Kross' body at the sensation of my touch.

"I know you love Mexican food, so I had Cactus deliver like ten minutes before you got here."

Lifting a brow, Kross peeked under the food cover.

"I wouldn't have known this was delivery since you put it on your good china," she badgered referring to the Tiffany plates I'd brought for Holly one year during Christmas. Since she was dealing with her dumb ass ex heavy and they broke everything they owned, I thought it would be best to keep them for myself.

Ready to eat, Kross excused herself, going into the house to wash her hands. When she returned and steadied across from me, I addressed what I knew was important.

"Kross, what I did was foul as fuck and I apologize. Not many women challenge me the way you do and I guess the coward in me decided to make my feelings for you something to laugh about. I'm a grown-ass man, I should've handled things differently."

"You damn right," she approved, slanting her head playfully while covering her lower half with a napkin.

"I like you Kross and I don't like people, "I started, taking a sip from my glass. I knew what I was about to share required a quenched palate and a clear mind.

Holding her chest dramatically, Kross forged surprise.

"Wow, I guess I should jump across the table and into your lap for the accomplishment, huh? You know, since I'm so special," she mocked, cutting into her Flautas.

"I'm not saying that. I just want you to understand me liking you is something worth knowing. The consistency of my feelings for you is the closest I've felt to love."

"Bullshit," she laughed.

"Wow, remind me to never tell you nothing."

"You're thirty-one, with a kid. You're telling me you never loved Connor's mom or any woman for that matter? That's bogus," she screeched, her top lip hitched.

"Do you want me to answer because you responded like you have the right to evaluate my feelings," I noted, reaching over and sticking a piece of shrimp from my fajitas in her mouth. Kross not questioning my actions was evidence of her comfort level with me increasing. I promised myself when I sent her gifts for a week straight, she'd have no reason to change the tempo, again.

"You're right, Hollis. Go ahead," she instructed with a curved smile.

"Ciara and I got together before either of us were ready to be committed or parents. I was fresh out, juggling two jobs and she was finding compassion elsewhere. After a while, it was an entitlement that kept us together, not the way we felt about each other. I loved her but never was in love. Real love isn't of convenience."

"I can respect that. Hell, I've been there. Can hardly tell the difference between intuition and insecurities."

"Exactly. Ciara didn't require much and at twenty-two, I needed that. Shit was hard too often at the time," I declared, damn near choking on my demons flooding above the routine I'd established.

"When I was younger, my sister's best friend and I started messing around. I was twelve, she was nineteen," I rambled off before I lost the balls to show Kross some of my hurt.

Shuffling in her chair, her already chinky eyes shaped. "What the hell?!"

Versus reacting to her outburst, I sustained before I shut down. I hadn't told this story, ever and repeating it now felt just as harsh as I thought it would.

"During the time, I swore I was falling in love and didn't care who had a problem with it. Kelsey didn't either until the secret got out. It had been five years since we started sleeping together and when my mother found out, she had a fucking fit. I knew things would be hard for us, even with the morally unsettling details of our relationship, but I had faith in us. When my mom confronted Kelsey and she got to talking, I realized there was no relationship. By that time the woman I thought loved me turned twenty-four, she'd become an elementary school teacher and unbeknownst to me, engaged to a whole other nigga. My mom was raising Holly and I alone, and didn't have many resources, so she decided to call the police. Kelsey was charged with engaging in sexual acts with a minor.

"Wow, that's fucking deep," Kross uttered, her mouth parted.

"Yeah, it was bad. Like you've said, Colten is a small city.

Imagine being seventeen with muthafuckas pressing you because your mom calls the cops for you gettin' pussy. Shit was hell. The bullying was more chaotic than my Mama's threatens, so I walked my black ass on the stand and didn't say a mumbling word."

"Wait, so you didn't testify?"

"Nah, I couldn't," I told her frankly. "Though Kelsey played me, I couldn't do the same. It wouldn't have made me feel any better and it wouldn't have brought us back together. After the case, I started to feel like I had to prove my manhood since everyone wanted to test it. I started hanging with the wrong crowd, got into trouble and ended up in jail for robbery."

"Did your mom forgive you for not speaking up? I know she was pissed when you didn't say anything after she went hard for you."

Glaring away from Kross, I thought about the relationship my mom and I now shared. I recalled her having to put her house up for my bail and me still running rapid. She went from protecting her child the prey, to defending her kid, the predator.

Unclear myself, I was truthful with Kross. "I'm not really sure."

"I guess, I'm not the only one with some issues. Is what you just shared the reason why you date married women?"

"Damn, straight shot," I spat, holding my chest as if wounded. I hadn't been in the company of any of my usual friends since I started dating Kross but I knew she was being petty, bringing up shit she saw in my phone months ago. Though she wasn't all the way off target, Shelby still hadn't gotten the hint.

"It sounds to me like what you shared with Kelsey is exactly what the premise of love is built on, sacrifice and unity. Maybe it was on a one-way street, so you don't feel it deserves the acknowledgment. If you don't want to claim that, I'd say you're kinda like a virgin?"

Grilling her, I sipped from my glass. "The fuck?"

"I'm just saying, you've never been *in* love and in the event that you fall for me, I basically popped your cherry," she boasted like that shit made sense.

"You're goofy," I teased. "I like it though."

"Look, I don't want to spend the entire evening revisiting things we can't change. We like each other, we're both a little screwed up but over nearly four months, things have just worked. I wouldn't be here if I wasn't ready to forgive you. Just don't let that shit happen again," she directed, adding firmness to a part of me I wanted her to feel.

"One more thing. Watch yourself and the company you keep. You may not be worried about the homes you've intruded on but believe me; some people are crazier than you think. Trust me, I've experienced one of them," she muttered in a shallow exhale.

Knowing exactly what she was referring to and feeling like shit that I was the anchor to those thoughts, I stood and walked to where she sat.

"Kross, look at me."

The way her eyes soared up almost stuttered my words.

"Regardless of the childish move I made, I haven't entertain another woman since you opened the door for the first time."

She disconnected at the revelation.

"Do you think I'd let someone hurt you?" I asked, pulling Kross up from her seat and wrapping my arms around her waist. Like a perfect piece, she melted into my grasp naturally.

Taking longer than I'd like, Kross shook her head. "No, but—"

"But, nothing. This is new for me, just like you. I need you to have faith in me, Kross. That's always been a disconnect for me and the woman I've been with. They don't trust that I could give them all they need. First Kelsey, then Ciara. I don't want that with you."

Giggling, Kross' fingers strummed the gold choker accenting her outfit choice.

"You were committed when your partners weren't, so you put yourself in situations where a commitment wasn't an option and her leaving is expected. The difference between then and now is, I'm not going anywhere," she teased.

Seeing her eyes spark under the overhead lights led me to

squeeze her tighter. Her body was heated, her eyes anticipating something I couldn't see.

"I'm screwed up, Hollis. I'm a twenty-eight-year-old woman that is anxious around people at times. I can barely boil water, I'm physically scarred and believe it or not, I've only been in love once. You sure this is what you want?" she quickly asked, carting away a bit of the ego she'd flashed moments ago.

"I know all that you've been through, Kross. I just don't give a fuck," was my rationale. "I'm still figuring things out myself but I'm not fearful of learning who you are now or who you want to be. I may not understand everything but I'm willing to love you even when I don't understand you."

"How do you know? We've known each other less than six months, Hollis."

"Me still being around with no pussy is how I know," I admitted. "Nothing you say will change my mind. I know where I wanna be; sounds like you're the one who hasn't figured it out yet."

"Is it okay if I figure it out *while* we enjoy one another?" she proposed.

Blushing like a broad in heat, I pressed our chest together. "I don't see a damn thing wrong with that."

"Can we figure it out, up there?" she marveled, pointing to Connor's oversized, overpriced treehouse.

"Will you be my friend again if I say yes?"

"Yep," she purred, licking her lips before grazing mine with her manicured fingernail.

"Let's roll then."

CHAPTER Fourteen

KROSS

"I can't believe I let you convince me to get up here. It's been damn near two months since Connor has been able to," Hollis criticized once situated in the miniature duck-off. Tonight, wasn't my first time at his home but it was the first time I'd enjoyed his backyard. I almost fainted taking in the dark red orchids and lights garnishing the area. Hollis was a manly man; so to have streamers, lights and pretty elements floating around his sanctuary meant a lot.

Tuning in to his grumbles, I walked over to the window. "And I can't believe you convinced me to come over, so I guess we're even."

"Man, I thought we were above all that. That was the deal if I brought you up here." Cringing, Hollis shook his head.

"Maybe that was the wrong choice of words."

Dramatically, I rolled my eyes. "Yea, I think you may be right."

Reaching out, I'd barely touched a figurine Connor had on display and Hollis' voice was elevating to its normal brash tone.

"Aye watch your hands. Connor would have a fit if she knew

we were all in her shit. She doesn't care about her own room more than this damn treehouse. It's all she requested when I had foundations added to the property."

"Hell, if I'd done all this work to make this place look like a single in the middle of SoHo, I'd be particular too."

The walls were decorated with photos of some of her favorite actresses and singers; just like my home, there were lights scattered across the pointed roof. Connor had everything from blankets to books in her kid cave and although Hollis said he wasn't a fan, he fit contentedly at 6 foot 6 in the wooden structure.

Staring out the window void of a screen, the patchy sky brought thoughts of other flaws I hadn't shared with Hollis. The physical scars that made moving on without reminders, impossible.

"Kross, tell me what you're thinking."

Resting my chin on my chest, I unconstrained my worry, allowing it to drift into the night breeze.

"That this may not work and it may be my fault. And though I said things with us are different from what I've ever given a chance, things may end up the same."

"But it's not supposed to be. Failure should never be the expectation." Seeing me losing my grip again, the forward man warmed my frame with his embrace.

"There has to be an expectation for greatness, or you'll always anticipate bullshit. You'll hang around until it emerges because you're expecting it."

Huffing, I titled my head. "I guess, you're right. Not like I haven't experienced it."

"You referring to ol' boy who couldn't cut it?" Hollis hissed like he'd experienced Roland's neglect firsthand.

Nodding, I squeezed my body close recalling when my solace became unsettling.

"Roland was one of the only men in *Body* who I knew before I started... taking dates. He worked for my parents on the legal end, so our connection was in place beforehand. Even when I made the decision to go partial, he—"

"Wait," Hollis interrupted. "What does partial mean?"

"It means I never went all the way with clients. Everything was done from the waist up. Sometimes no sexual activities at all," I explained.

"Aww, hell nah. Niggas were really paying you to look at your face?"

"Sometimes," I flushed.

Shaking his head, Hollis smacked my ass. "Nah, Imma need to see more than that."

"Shut up!" I elbowed him, a grin that I couldn't drop, plastered.

"It's crazy, I was worth all the trouble that came with loving a woman who worked in a whore house but Roland didn't think I was worth the trouble when I needed him most. Most of his life, he'd been treated like a second-class nerd. Even when he acquired a little money, women didn't want to date the little man with confidence issues and decent pockets; but I was okay with it. He was nice, ambitious, and even if I never fell *in* love, I knew I'd be taken care of. It didn't occur to me that he lacked the ability to take care of my heart until that became the priority. Until my pockets were laced and the only thing I required was his existence. That was too much for Roland. He didn't know how to conceal his disgust when looking at my burns and his anger just festered when he couldn't get me to speak. That bastard had this sick gratitude for my profession. In his mind, it was sort of 'the nerd gets to fuck the head cheerleader' vibe. It was all good until I walked away with remnants of the fire. That's when my appeal decreased and so did his presence."

"Damn, that's foul. I mean, I don't know what you looked like before but you're gorgeous now. That nigga was never in it for the long haul if that's all it took for him to walk away."

"Honestly, we both had ulterior motives when being together. Roland wanted a trophy wife and I wanted stability," I unveiled.

"How'd you get the scars?"

After reminding myself that I was safe, I answered. "A fire I was involved in. My client's wife lost her shit and came to the place with guns blazing. She thought it would be more gratifying to have me burn alive. The damage on my upper thighs and ass could've been way worst."

"You're a survivor," he spoke into the night, sounding so sure and confident in the allegation.

"Hardly."

"What do you want now, Ms. Peach Street?" Hollis inquired, his body pressing against mine. His being here brought relief I could adore forever and lose myself within; I was over fighting it too. The heat of his breath coating my collar triggered my eyes to shut and my mind to open.

"Tell me, Kross. What do you want? Where do you want to be?"

"Somewhere safe," I countered, orbs hardly visible as they struggled to stay zoned. My frame, cravings, and thirst were going crazy at the vibration of his respire finding my skin.

Deciding to divulge it all and premiere evidence of my survival, I pushed Hollis back.

"I want to show you something," I proposed.

"Okay," he responded, never dropping his eyes while sitting on an oversized bean bag. Petrified to lose the courage, I unzipped my dress and allowed it to fall to the floor. I thought it was cute that Hollis was detaining his eyes from roaming anywhere other than my expression.

"You're so goofy," I said, unable to block my childish leer from invading our supposedly serious moment.

"I'm being serious, Hollis."

"Me too, shit. I don't know how much longer I can look at that mug with that body out but I'm trying to be a gentleman, woman," he taunted, his long legs taking up a lot of floor space.

"Every day I wake with these reminders of my actions; of the hurt I caused and then received in return. The brothel, the men, and the scars; it's all me."

"You talking to me or the floor?" he searched, making my gaze find his as my feet ushered my frame to his positioning.

"You. I'm talking to you," I flirted, straddling his lap with my clothed chest pressed against his and my scarred thighs on display. When Hollis' hungrily latched on to my blackened thigh, I flinched.

"You scared of me?"

"No. There's no reason to be," I shot back, firm on my statement. "I wouldn't be here if I was scared of you, I am scared of *us*. Even with how much I want you."

Removing my busied hair from out of my face, Hollis kissed the parts of me that he couldn't keep his hands off of. First my chin and then my forehead was in receipt of his affection. Pulling my shirt over my head, I returned the favor and assisted him in doing the same.

"I won't lie, my patience for shit I don't get has never been the most solid. But leaving isn't an option, especially not for you remaining exactly who you've been from the jump," he promised, licking the center of my chest like something sweet resided.

"I know what I'm getting into and that shit ain't movin' me, Kross."

Like we'd waited our entire lives for this moment, Hollis and I kissed as if we'd finally arrived. We went from sudden pecks to wet exchanges that I could feel between my legs. My pussy was soak at the thought of how good Hollis would feel.

Deciding to take control, Hollis softly pushed me down so that I was laying on my back.

"Everything about you is beautiful to me," he adored, unsnapping my bra and filling the space with his lips.

"You really thought a war wound would change the way I feel about you? The way I see you?" Hollis demanded to know. When his tongue massaged below my belly button, I became even more eager for his touch and less aware of my own reactions.

"Mhm, your lips feel so good," I purred, taking a handful of his twisted hair into my palm. I couldn't help the grin I wore hearing Hollis laugh at my movement. It had been a year since I had dick that didn't require batteries, and honestly I'd be fantasizing about Hollis' rude ass since he made it clear he wanted to eat me alive.

"If you want me to eat this pussy just say so, Kross."

Relinquishing any reservations, I asked for what I wanted. I was done debating or being coy with my omissions. I wanted Hollis to make love to me and that's what I expected him to do.

"Hollis, I want you to eat my pussy like it's the best pie you've ever had in your life. I want you to get nasty and sloppy like the day you were eating that fucking peach on my porch."

Hearing Hollis growl and feeling him nip on the inside of my thighs as I spoke had me stuttering. When my moans morphed into purring, Hollis gripped my ass.

"Keep talkin' that nasty shit," he ordered, licking from the back of my jewel to the front.

"I can't take the teasing, Hollis. Just fuck me like you're mad I've been away so long then make love to me like we'll live in the sensation forever."

Showcasing strength that was apparent by simply looking at him. Hollis tightened the hold he had on my waist and thigh. Within a blink of an eye, I was positioned bare ass and spread eagle in what I knew to be a reading chair.

No words were spoken; nothing except for my cries of pleasure and Hollis' admiration for me allowing him to taste me.

"Fuck Hollis. I'm about to cum!"

Reaching up, he stuck his finger in my mouth. The entire time my juices ran down his throat, I sucked on his finger like it were the hard-on he'd pulled out and couldn't help stroking.

"Yes," I cooed.

"That's right. Let that shit go," he encouraged making my body hover even higher than where it set.

~ Once I found my sense of gravity, I pushed Hollis back to the seat he'd initially occupied.

Greedily, I ridded his face of my juice. "You nasty as fuck"
I giggled.

"Nah. Don't play shy now. I like that shit," he professed, taking my bottom lick into his mouth with his teeth. Never breaking our kiss, I reached down between us and grab a handful of Hollis's dick. My mouth watered feeling strong veins protrude and the head sparkle because of my touch.

"You're so big," I whispered, not giving a damn how thirsty I sounded. The smirk on his face let me know he didn't mind.

"Feel big too. Put it in," he commanded. And like an obedient fein, I slid Hollis inside of me.

"Ah, yes, baby," I purred, my raspy speech becoming light.

"You wet as fuck, Kross. Shit," he chanted, smacking my ass as I grind my pelvis into his. The feeling of my clit and pussy both getting a dose of perfect pressure, had my head back and my mouth open.

Squeezing my ass cheeks that fit in the palm of his hands like flawless fixtures, I threw my head back as I rode my wave.

"Harder," I instructed, prompting the beast who matched my stigma to grip my flesh tighter.

"Your pussy wrapping around me like it's mine," he murmured.

"Hollis, I've been waiting to feel you, baby," I admitted, bringing my body closer to his. Draping my arms around his neck, I cooed at the freedom overtaking his demeanor.

"You ready to love me?" he asked. It was the cutest thing, having a man as big as him fawning over my feelings and not just my body.

Licking his lips, I narrowed my gaze. "It's too late. I already do."

"I can feel that shit. Every time I see you, touch you, and smell you it's confirmation that this is real. Fuck, you feel good," he spat as if disgusted with me for having something so addictive at my disposable.

Grinding my hips into him, I moaned like crazy basking in our love. Rubbing a hand up and down his hard stomach, I hissed feeling myself about to cream.

"Baby keep doing that," I pleaded, recognizing the way his hips rotated in perfect rhythm beneath me.

"How does this dick feel?"

"Like it belongs to me; like something I can get used to," I crowed, not giving a damn who heard or who didn't agree. Hollis and I had certainly drifted into bounds outside of platonic, I knew there was no going back. I didn't want to.

CHAPTER Fifteen

HOLLIS

The word proud didn't hold enough validity to express the joy I felt watching my baby on stage. Connor had been practicing for her big day for months and her work was visible. Everything from the way she pronounced her lines with confidence to the tone she'd used when singing Nina Simone's *'Don't Let Me Be Misunderstood'*, Connor delivered a beautiful performance. I would've called the entire night perfect had her momma not been in the audience hooting like she didn't have any damn sense. If Ciara wasn't screaming that the brown-skin beauty was her kid, she was ice grilling Kross who set beside me like Ciara wasn't in the room. I knew Kross being here was only for Connor, all the extra drama Ciara was sprawling she could keep.

I was courteous enough to tell her beforehand that I was bringing Kross and she pretending it was no big deal. Nevertheless, from the moment me and my girl walked in hand and hand, Ciara had been mugging us like we owed her money. When I saw one of her hoodrat friends sitting beside her, I knew the night would be long.

"Girl, ain't nobody worried about her baldheaded-ass. Just like every other one, she'll be Gone with the Wind soon. Mark my words," Ciara swore, doing an awful job at whispering her insult.

Sick of the hissing, I turned to tell Ciara about herself.

"Aye, watch your—"

"Maybe if you paid closer attention to your daughter as opposed to what's flying in the wind, you wouldn't have to call your kid's dad to get the details for your baby's performance. Don't get it misunderstood, I'm baldhead by choice. That long hair shit is played, just like the light skin trait doesn't make you cute. Now keep your eyes off of me before I give you something to really look at, duck," Kross warned , cutting me off and shutting Ciara up.

"Mmm, you know I like that bossy, shit," I mumbled in her ear. Shoving me away, Kross told me to focus on the show and kept a sly grin on her face the rest of the time.

Nearly an hour later, we were rushing up over to the star of the night with flowers and gifts. None the wiser, Connor ran up to us but instantly jumped in Kross' arms.

"You did such a good job, puddin'. The steps and the singing were on point. Plus, you didn't stumble over one line," Kross boasted, placing Connor back on her feet.

"Thank you! Thank you! I—"

"Connor!" Ciara yelled, motivating eyes to fall on our circle. "You don't see anybody else here? Your Aunty Fancy came to see you and you just ignore her?"

"That's not my auntie," Connor clowned under her breath.

Moving to snatch her up, I interfered before she could touch my kid.

"Aye, back the hell up. Did you forget where you are? Somebody at this damn school will call CPS on you, then what? Use your head," I snapped. When I felt Kross' fingers squeeze mine, I calmed myself.

Stepping in my face, Ciara's mean expression mirrored mine. "Don't tell me how to be a damn mother when you have some broad around my daughter that you know won't last. You've never been this messy, Hollis."

"Ciara, you're mad because you know my relationship with Kross is anything but a flock. That shit gets under your skin! Get over it! She hasn't done shit to you so stop acting like she has." Refusing to argue with her, I cut off Ciara's rebuttal and turned to Connor.

"Baby girl, you going with me or your mom?" Walking over, she hugged me around my waist.

"I'm going to go with mommy tonight."

Barking inwardly, I nodded.

"Bet. Call me when you're ready to come home."

"She's going home," Ciara blurted.

Tuning her out, I kneeled in front of Connor, so we were eye level. "Call me if you need me. Me, not granny. You hear me?"

"Yes sir," she beamed. Kissing her goodbye, I didn't offer Ciara another word as Kross and I exited the building.

"You did good in there," I admired, recalling how calm she'd been during the performance. Between the speakers spazzing and the random clapping, I didn't know if Kross would be able to hang the entire night.

"Are you talking about the crowd or your ratchet ass baby mama?" she quizzed, touching her chin with her index finger.

"Both."

"Hmm, well, thank you. The crowd was small and it seemed the more I focused on Connor, the more I was able to tune the audience out. She really is talented and as long as she says consistent, she can have whatever she wants from the music world. You know she's been writing songs and texting them to me for my opinion?" Kross bragged like Connor was her kid and not mine.

"You over there glowing talking about the kid. You can adopt her if you'd like," I teased.

Becoming coy, Kross relaxed in her seat.

"Don't act all shy. I think it's beautiful how much you and Connor vibe. It's actually a blessing. Her approval means the world to me," I told her, reaching over and squeezing her thigh.

Blushing, Kross grabbed my hand and kiss it with her eyes closed.

"What was that for?"

"For always talking me off the ledge," she answered.

Chuckling, I glanced at Kross. "I'm supposed to do that for *you*."

"Oh, I know, but there are no roles in this love thang, baby," she stated.

"Love?"

"That's what I said," Kross moved like she hadn't just said a mouthful. I knew the sensation wasn't just wordplay either. I was exactly where she was on the spectrum of feelings.

Pulling up to Kross' house, we both mumbled aloud seeing a man standing on her porch with flowers in his clutch. Ol' boy wasn't wearing a Brown Brothas uniform, so he couldn't have been making a delivery. That meant he shouldn't have been on Kross' porch.

My first thought was to accuse her of some foul shit. Cheating was the pattern of the women I dated. Yes, I knew Kross wasn't like anyone I'd fallen for and yes, Ciara had done enough barking throughout night for all of us. Yet, the real nigga in me wouldn't allow that to be enough to silence my concern.

"Who is that?"

She said nothing.

"You don't want to answer? Want me to figure it out on my own?" I fished, my heart thumping harder the longer she stayed quiet.

Waving my hand in her face, I repeated myself. "Hello. You don't hear me?"

"Stop freaking yelling at me, Hollis!"

"Kross, trust me. I'm not yelling. Just answer the damn question. Please."

Sighing, she unhooked her seatbelt but didn't move to get out.

"That's Roland, my ex and before you start having a fit, no I didn't know he'd be here. I would never disrespect you by entertaining another man and I think you know that. I haven't talked to that man in almost a year. I don't know why he's here, Hollis."

"You want to find out?"

Staring at her house guest, Kross shook her head.

"Not really," she clarified, protecting her body with crossed arms. Letting down my passenger window, I called out to the idiot pacing her porch with roses in his hands. Fuck boy didn't know Kross doesn't like roses?

"Aye, jackass, you looking for Kross?" I called out.

"Oh my god," Kross groaned, sinking in her seat like a child embarrassed by their obnoxious parent.

"Yeah. Are you a friend of hers?" he had the nerve to ask.

"Nah, I'm her nigga."

Boastful, the idiot had the nerve to laugh. Cutting my eyes, I grimaced seeing him pull out his phone like he was about to call her.

"I know that foo' ain't about to call you," I garbled looking between him and the woman I was ready to go to war for. I knew enough about the clown to know none of what he did was from a genuine narrative. If that nigga was showing up, he wanted something.

Reaching out, I lifted Kross' chin so it was positioned like there was a crown on her head.

"Sit up and lift your head. You never hide from anyone, especially not with me at your side," I bustled, grinning when corny caught a glimpse of Kross' pretty ass in the passenger side of my car. It was obvious Urkel was still sorting through the scene.

Walking slowly in our direction, I barked, making him flinch. Kross' laugh caused my serious face to break.

"If you walk over here, you're a fool. Neither you nor those dry ass flowers could change her mind. Shit was too much for you and you took too long to right your wrongs. Bust a move," I advised, pulling off with him still trying to fully dissect the notion that he'd lost his girl.

"Oh my God! You're crazy!" Kross yelled in between giggles. Cute, girl giggles that made men my size crumpled on command when they spilled from the right woman.

"Where are we headed, Ms. Peach Street?"

"Doesn't matter. Wherever you are, that's where I'll be," she replied, words pulling my eyes to hers with no resistant.

"Hmm, is that right."

"Yep," she sassed, popping glossed lips for emphasis.

Sliding a hand between Kross' legs like we hadn't just had two run-ins that could've turned our night to shit, I rubbed on the sweet area I'd been having a field day inside since our reconciliation.

"I wanna go somewhere nasty," I told her. Slipping her bottom lip between her teeth for relief, Kross moaned her reply.

"Moan again if that's a yes," I teased, palming her clothed pussy. With her head rested against her seat, the ignited freak reached over and returned the gesture.

"Damn," I grumbled, doing my best to steer the car and enjoy her touch. Kross was winning the concentration for my attention.

When she pulled my dick from my slacks, I knew we wouldn't make it home.

"Don't pull over," Kross instructed, kissing the tip of my dick like it was something worthy of time.

"I won't be able to concentrate on the side of a dark road," she reiterated since I'd forgotten that fast.

"I know your mental is strong enough to do two things at one time. I think you can take it," she encouraged, covering me before I had time to prepare myself.

"Fuck. Suck that shit den," I uttered, using one hand to guide her head while the other rested on the steering wheel. I didn't want to bust fast or in Kross' mouth, but the way she was swirling her tongue, and massaging my balls, there was no guarantee.

"Swallow it," I told her, and obediently she did. Glaring up from my lap, Kross rubbed her teeth against the head with the perfect amount of pressure when I became too relaxed.

"Uh, Uh. Watch the road. It's not that good."

"Nah, it's better than good. You gon' make me bust in yo' mouth," I lauded, with no gas.

Hearing how turned on Kross was from giving me pleasure, took my prominent anticipation to another level.

"That moaning is making my pussy wet."

"Fuck," I blurted, happy as hell when I turned on my street.

"I can't wait to feel that pussy wrap around all this dick you wettin' up."

Putting my car in park, Kross slowly released me from her mouth. Again, she did that pop noise that made my dick jump. Hopping out the driver's side, I didn't bother to button my pants as I went over to Kross' door. Gently, I grabbed the freaky fein from her seat and situated her legs around my waist.

"If you don't stop giggling, I'm going to drop you."

"You should've buttoned your pants," she taunted.

"No need. As soon as we get through that door, I'm on you." I smirked seeing goosebumps perforate on her skin at my warning.

Stroking the back of my neck, Kross blushed. "You gotta catch me first."

"Bet. I'll even give you a head start," I replied, sitting her on her feet once I got the door open.

"Hollis, I was just joking we are not about to play hide and go get it. We are too old for that," she scolded.

"One, two, three…," I started counting and smirked wickedly when she kicked off her boots and took off running into my backyard.

CHAPTER Sixteen

Hollis

"My Daddy called me again."

Guiding our bikes down the boardwalk, I stayed quiet until she required my response.

"He wants me to come back to work for *Body*. They're opening back up in a few weeks."

"How do you feel about that," I asked.

"I feel like it's bullshit. I'm not going back. My business is doing well and I don't think he's taking that well."

Pulling her to me by the waist, I absorbed Kross' ass settled in black cargo pants; her upper body cover by an Ari Lennox graphic tee that stopped above her navel.

"We don't have to talk about shit that's not important. You're a grown ass woman; you have the right to distinguish what's best for you. As a parent, he should respect that."

Leaning her head to the side, Kross grinned like she saw me through new eyes.

"You're right."

"Damn right. Now let's get back to our lesson. That's a damn shame. Your parents taught you how to count money in a brothel but didn't include simple shit like riding a bike?"

Resting her hand on her hips, the scowl Kross had in placed deepened. "Are you going to teach me or keep making me feel small?"

Feeling the extent of my jokes hitting harder than intended, I snuggled up to Kross. The pout she wore was a clear indicator that I'd said too much.

"I'm sorry, I didn't mean any harm. You know I was just talking shit." Instead of speaking, Kross snatched away. Pressing her ass against me while staring out at the ocean water. The sun was just rising but thanks to the unpredictable weather the breeze was warm.

"Can you stop looking at me like that and do like I asked."

"If you stop talking shit, I'd probably do just about anything you say," she mumbled, thin eyes now casing over a handful of morning cyclists.

It took less protest than I expected to not only convince Kross to come outside but also to visit Venice Beach with me. The landmark was usually packed but considering the time of day, I knew it would be a ghost town.

Hearing Kross' request for a gentler approach, I chilled my barking and gave the lady what she deserved.

Deliberately, I moved Kross' body so close to mine there was so no way we weren't exchanging the same inhale.

"Nah, don't get cute now," she whispered, cheeks rising so high they turned her eyes into slits.

"I don't mean to come off as harsh. That's just my delivery. It's not a measurement of my patience with you. I think you know that by now though. Believe it or not, I'm the calmest with you and Connor," I ensured her. "This isn't a game for me."

"Ha! Guess, you just forgot all about betting on—"

Smacking her ass, I cut off her unsettling recollection.

"Why you gotta bring up old shit?" I tested, sharing the same warm smile she wore. At this point, I was no longer concerned with her rejection, our titles or my trust issues. We spent time together at least four times a week and been fucking like animals since the first time in Connor's treehouse. Though we both were invested in furthering our business ventures, that did nothing to deter the interest we had in one another.

"I want you to think of this how you've been preparing for that charity event coming up."

Kross had been invited by the Cali Buzz to speak at a women's event. All the speakers were survivors and locals and they'd asked Kross to come share her story. She'd been doing different exercises with Dr. Sway to get ready for the big day. I was proud that she accepted the invitation.

Squeezing her legs, I prompted Kross' eyes to find mine. "You comfortable?"

"Yes," she huffed, her concern on display.

"Even if you fall, I'll be right here to get you," I promised, pulling her face to mine for a kiss. "Now, I want you to put your feet on the petal just as I showed you and push off. You said you've been cycling before, so it should be easy."

Nodding, Kross stammered. "Okay. Okay, I can do this."

"You don't have a choice," I said, staring a hole in the side of her face while jogging at her side. Giving her a few minutes to gain her balance, I warned Kross of my next move.

"Oh my God! Hollis! You better not let me fall!" The short hair beauty screamed freely in between giggles and nervousness.

"Bae, keep your feet on the pedals, guide the handles and you'll be just fine," I directed. Like a good girl, she did as I said and gripped the handlebars with precision.

"Good girl. Now, put those strong ass legs to work," I teased holding onto the padded seat with one hand and planting a kiss on the back of Kross' neck.

"You better stop," she murmured. Just as her eyes began to shut, Kross playfully shoved me away.

"Stop trying to screw me and get back to our lesson," she advised, peaking at me over her shoulder with something other than just admiration covering her expression.

"See. I told you it wasn't that hard. Gotta trust yourself," I coached but swallowed the revelation myself. I don't know how this woman made me fein for shit I was good without but I was stuck. Everything about her growth stimulated me, when before I didn't want to be attached unless below the waist. Having *only* that type of interaction felt like cheating myself when the woman had way more to offer.

"Keep pedaling!"

"Hollis," she called out between laughs, she couldn't control.

"You got it, bae," I encouraged, my fingers slowly slipping from her seat.

"Don't let me go, Hollis," she begged, voice morphing from hyped to hectic.

"I promise, you got this! Keep moving your feet, I got yo back."

Though she shouldn't have, Kross glared at me. Wetness slid down her face as I let her go.

"That's right! That's what I'm talking about," I boasted, happy as hell when Kross kept the bike steady without my assistance.

"I love you, Hollis," she shouted, sun rays reflecting on her skin burned the memory into my recall.

Hopping on the bike I'd dropped to the side, I pedaled fast catching up to an emotional Kross. By the time I got to her side, she was still maintaining her balance, with tears dropping. I didn't need to ask for the root, she was happy.

Glancing over, I smiled when she snorted at her own sensitivity.

"I love you too, Kross. Like for real, I love you," I confessed, relief engulfing my chest once I admitted the notion.

Nearly two hours later, I was returning our rentals while Kross continued to mention how much she wanted stuffed French Toast and bacon.

"Man, I told you about eating that pork," I teased, always messing with her and her warped eating habits. I'd never meant anyone who loved bacon as much as Kross.

Jumping on my back, the laid back pest flicked my ear with her finger.

"We already talked about this . I'm a pork eater and you eat my pussy, so what does that make you?"

"Starving from this point forward," I clowned, taking off into a jog through the parking lot like a fool in love with a tickled Kross on my back. My amazement was just as loud as hers and my heart escalated at the sensation of her thighs in my hold and her arms wrapped around my neck for support.

"Are you going to get Connor?"

Twisting my lips, I gave Kross a knowingly look. "I don't know. I don't feel like listening to you two pretend to be Sunny and Cher all night. She's only been on winter break a hot second and y'all are already driving me up a wall."

Nibbling on my ear lightly, Kross purred. "You wanted me to come outside, now what are you going to do with me?" Sounding just as I had when I said it to her; I couldn't help but blush at her mockery.

"Sometimes I forget your daddy's a pimp and your mama's good looking," I mentioned, groaning when she nudged my ribs.

Only a few feet away from my car, I placed Kross on her feet when noticing some stranger sitting on the hood of my Benz like he'd lost mind.

"Who the hell is he?" Kross mumbled, stepping behind me even though I had already positioned myself as a safeguard.

"Man, you must want yo ass beat sitting on my shit like you don't have any sense," I hollered, pulling up my sweats as we got closer. Putting my hand up, I signaled for Kross to hand back a bit.

"Mr. Hollis Brown?" The tall man tested giving no indication of who *he* was.

"Yeah, what's up?"

"Mr. Brown, you've been served."

Taking the envelope, the messenger handed off, I waited until he was out my face and I'd gotten Kross in the car prior to ripping it open.

Scanning over the content fast, I growled, balling the memo's edges the further down I read.

"What the fuck!" I blurted, reading the child support notice but not at all receiving that shit well.

CHAPTER Seventeen

HOLLIS

"You sure you gon' be good man? I haven't seen you this faded since the first time you drank," Rock clowned, pulling into my driveway after I'd had more liquor than my tolerance was built for.

"Man, I'm a grown-ass man. I can handle my shit," I swanked, undoing my seatbelt and pushing my door open with unnecessary force.

"I do appreciate you going out with me and listening to all my baby mama drama and chaos. I can't believe that bitch, man," I objected, getting vexed hastily. Pulling out my phone, I squeezed the device seeing the blocked number flash. I knew it was Shelby's stalking ass still pressing me to talk. After seven months of no dick and very little conversation, her obsession was now just overkill.

"Man, you have all your affairs in order and a place for your daughter to lay her head happily that's more secure than anything Ciara has going. I'm telling you there's nothing for you to worry about."

Rubbing my hand down the length of my face, I breathed out air-filled of whiskey and worries.

"You want me to call Kross to come down," Rock quizzed.

"Nigga!" I barked, pointing my finger between his eyes. "Don't ever talk to my lady. I know you don't got her number." I tested, snatching his phone from his possession. Taking it back, Rock laughed like I was a damn joke.

"You buggin'," he taunted, purposely trying to get under my skin while he could.

"Besides, she's supposed to be in bed, naked with that damn guitar wrapped around her body, not coming down to get me," I shouted, leaving his door wide open and his mouth running.

Stumbling through my front door, I dropped my keys in the foyer and my work jacket in the hall.

"Bae," I called out. I knew she hadn't gone home considering all the damn lights in the house were on.

"Kross. I know you ain't sleep bae," I persisted, sliding in bed behind her. Like always, she was wearing a pair of biker bottoms and one of my nightshirts.

Moving around, I could smell the fresh shower drift from her skin. When Kross rolled over, I followed her gesture.

"Mmm, what are you doing?"

I didn't reply, just rubbed her nipples between the balls of my fingers. The combination of the mint body wash Kross liked to use and her natural scent had me grinding across her body like I was already inside. Pulling her closer, I wrapped one head around her chest while the other snaked between her legs.

"Hollis, you're drunk. What the hell?" Ignoring her this time, I gradually trailed my fingers up and down the inside of her thigh.

"Damn, you smell good," I told her, placing kisses at the top of her spine.

"Ahhh, Hollis. I don't want to do this while you're drunk. You don't even drink," she recognized. When I didn't take heed, she became more firm.

"Hollis. I'm serious. No." The tone of Kross' voice echoed throughout my eardrums causing me to jump. Even fucked up on Jameson and Coke, I could recognize fear when I heard it.

Removing my hands quickly, my chest tightened at the

thought of Kross being afraid of me. As if she sensed my dread, Kross rolled over so she was staring at the ceiling.

"Hollis, I'm—"

"You better not apologize. You didn't do anything wrong. If you say no, the answer is no."

Disregarding my comprehension, she explained whatever it was she felt needed to be said.

"Being intimate while you're in this mindset reminds me of my old life; of the men in the brothel sloppy drunk and unable to control themselves. I don't want that type of vibe for us."

"I told you, you didn't have to explain yourself, Kross," I answered back, shutting the door as I walked out on her.

Stumbling down my basement stairs I didn't bother turning on the light before allowing my body to loosen completely, crashing across the couch and shutting my eyes for a much needed break.

The next morning, my head was spinning, the same as my thoughts. In a hurry, I changed into a Nike track shirt and shorts, rushing out the door before Kross could wake up. The entire time I ran, I thought of Kross' voice when asking me for space. True, my demeanor was out of the ordinary but never would I cross the boundaries that she insinuated.

It took me longer than usual to get back home after circling the block and once I did, my focus rest on the punching bag I installed in my basement years ago. If I didn't find a way to free my anger before court in a few weeks, my true feelings for Ciara and her bullshit request would be on blast. I hadn't seen my daughter in days and childishly, her mother was hovering over her phone. One I pay the bill on, by the way. Ciara had always been a headache and I never believed she'd grow up. But I also didn't think her jealously stemming from me moving on would result in court papers and separation from my kid. Kross had been doing her best to level my head but between my nature to snap and hers to either go silent or return the aggression, it hadn't been as tension free as I would've liked.

Even when I saw the talented beauty tip-topped down my basement steps, I didn't discontinue my pounding. It had only been a week since Ciara had me served and I hadn't been out the house for shit other than drinks and work since. I could tell my demeanor was getting under Kross' skin but the solider in her was holding down the position at my side.

Sitting on the bottom stairs of a room I had converted into a small gym, the tolerant woman watched me somberly. Her elbows rested on her knees while her hands cradled her face. The part of me that loved her wanted to ask if she was okay. Her vibe was low and lately she'd been playing slow melodies. I knew my switch in energy was the cause and sadly, I still couldn't alter my mood.

After the radio went from bumping Weezy to E-40, Kross moved over to the boom box and turned it off.

Giving her a blank stare, I waited to hear whatever she needed to get off her chest.

"Do you want me to leave Hollis?" She spoke evenly, her fingers moving like her prized possession was in place.

Slowing my blows, I concentrated on the target. "Did I say that?"

"You didn't have to. You've been snapping, distant, and short. I don't know what that shit last night was. I've been around you for months and never saw you have a drink. If you need some space—"

I cut her off. "Look, if you want to leave don't ask me for permission. I'm not giving it to you, Kross. Is shit too heavy? You can admit that without my input."

"A house is supposed to be a sanctuary not a prison, Hollis. Shit is heavy here, you know that. I'm not saying I don't understand why, I'm just trying to get in your head because you're shutting me out and I don't like it," she spat.

"I'm surprised that would be a problem for you," I snarled, knowing I was wrong to throw that in her face.

"Hollis, that doesn't hurt me. If this is how you're going to fight in court then you may as well let Ciara have Connor. Is this really over Connor or is it a control thing like always," she stupidly commented, standing in my face with her fist in balls at her side.

"I'm not allowing that broad to have shit. She's doing this

because I have you now but you're crazy as hell to agree with her moves and say I should bow down. Are you crazy?" I hissed, knowing Kross meant no harm but unable to imprison my defenses.

"You have me confused with those dingbats who take the bare minimum from you with no rebuttal. I would never insinuate your baby isn't worth a fight. I'm just reminding you that you have to be present to fight for her. Stooping to Ciara's level makes you no better."

"How would you fucking know? You've said it yourself, you were spoiled and never had to fight for shit!"

"I had to fight for my sanity, nigga! My life! What the hell is wrong with you?"

"Us not being on the same page when the move should be obvious is what's wrong with me. You want me to just give my kid up? I'm not that type of man, Kross," I barked. "What you want me to shut the world out and cry about it like you? I can't do that."

"I never asked you to! I would never ask you to but I'm not going to tell you to go beat the girl up or act like a female because she's challenging you. Be a fucking man and fight for your kid the smart way," she screamed, tears rushing to her chin.

"Fucking asshole!" The hurt in her voice as she rushed up the stairs made me go to work on the bag all over again. Slamming the door as hard as she could, I only went up the stair once I heard the door seal.

A week of separation from Kross and a few necessary conversations with Holly had me seeking a stench of mental refuge I didn't think was required.

I knew it may have been pointless but I had one of my boys who ran background checks for Brown Brothas to check into Kelsey's last listed address. Out of everything Holly yelled during our bonding time one thing was for certain, I didn't have closure when it came to the betrayal of my first love. Up until a few months ago, I rarely claimed the broad.

Pulling up to the address forwarded to my email, I kept my car running as I watched the house I'd been directed to. The street was quiet and other than a few girls playing jump rope on the sidewalk there weren't many people out.

"Man, what the hell are you doing here?" I babbled aloud, taking my car out of park once the realization hit. Nevertheless, the vision of a woman I swore to never see again came into focal, halting my movements. She looked exactly how I remembered with red hair touching the middle of her back, and intrusive round eyes surveying the neighborhood. Without concern, the almost forty-year-old woman appeared happy. Not at all basing life's progression around something she'd done years ago. Kelsey didn't seem to need my blessing to move on with her life.

So why did I feel compelled to hear an apology in order to move on with mine?

CHAPTER Eighteen

KROSS

"I'm going to cut you off if you don't focus. I told you when you asked to stay over, you had to practice. I have a speech to go over, remember?"

Slouching in the side across from me, Connor poked out her lips.

"I'm trying," she whined. "But learning to play the guitar isn't easy."

"Oh really? I had no idea," I replied, squeezing her knee teasingly.

"You think you're going to be Jimi Hendrix after a day and it's not happening, princess," I told her, fidgeting with her rested chin.

"Did you call your dad?"

"Nope. I'll do that now," she urged, quick to release the instrument she wanted to master overnight. Coming back into my sights, Kross bounced my way.

"Yes, Auntie Holly dropped me off after Granny took me to her. And no, Kross is just nervous about her speech but she isn't mad at you."

"Don't talk about me like I'm not in the room. Stick to the code, girl!" I teased, walking away before Hollis could talk her into passing me the phone. I wasn't upset with him but I didn't want to particularly talk. We communicated here and there over the past two weeks and saw each other once but there was still something off. I didn't think he was cheating or seeing someone else but I did feel Hollis had some things on his heart that needed to be spoken aloud. I offered to schedule him an appointment with Dr. Sway but was met with reservations and gender role bullshit that pissed me off.

Running into the kitchen, Connor called my name. "Kross, catch!" Out of reflex, I lifted my hands and came down with her phone in my hold. I mean, I *was* wearing my Peyton Manning Jersey, but goodness.

"Really Connor?" I warned, seeing her daddy's big nose all in the lens.

"Sorry. He said he'd give me fifty bucks," she shrugged, her high ponytail bouncing with glee as she explained.

"Fifty?" I recited aloud, my eyes cutting to the roof of my house. "This *is* big money on the line."

"See!"

Snickering as Connor scurried out the kitchen, I purposely released a loud breath.

"Really? All that?"

Smacking my lips, I moved around the kitchen with the phone in one hand while I used the other to sort through take-out menus. "What do you want?"

"For you to stop being mean to me."

"I'm not being mean to you. I'm giving you the space I believe you need. You have court in a few weeks to sort out custody and the amount of support. I'm respecting your space."

Groaning, he moved the camera from his annoyed expression then refocused on himself.

"See, there you go again. Getting upset because you don't like what I'm saying." This man thought just because he voted in favor of gay rights and other liberal shit he was open-minded. His temperament said otherwise.

"Can we talk about this in person? We're not kids, Kross. I haven't seen you in days."

"Don't go there. You know Connor and I are chilling and ironically, there are no boys allowed," I announced, rejoining my bestie for the night.

"Girls only, daddy! Now, leave us alone. We're about to watch movies," she announced, making it known that we were done with practice for the night.

"I'll leave you guys be when Kross agrees to be my friend again."

Scoffing, my lip hitched. "I'm tired of forgiving you."

"Oh, well, I'm not going anywhere and I don't plan to become perfect, so you can get over that. We agreed to always meet in the middle, so where you at?"

"Hmm, I don't know," I replied, shrugged indifferently.

"Oh for real? You don't know? I can come in and show you. I'm outside," he revealed.

When my eyes grew wide, he smirked. "I'm wherever you are baby."

"Bye," I giggled, hanging up before I had to leave Connor to a solo girl's night.

Ding! Dong!

Damn near skipping to the living room, I didn't bother checking the camera before opening the door.

"Negro! Didn't I just tell you to leave us alon— Roland? What the hell are you doing here?" I muttered. Though he'd showed up to my door months ago, I hadn't seen him since.

"I came to see you. Happy you don't have your guard dog nearby this time," he commented. Assuming he was referring to Hollis, I frowned.

"He's actually about five minutes away, so you better make it quick," I embellished.

"Umm, who is this?" I heard a small voice wonder behind me. Glancing inside the house, Connor stood with a grimace covering her face.

"Go finish practicing and I'll be right back inside," I instructed.

"I'm going to tell my daddy," Connor yelled, right as my door shut.

"Wow, you're a mother now?" he tested mockingly. The same square glasses covered his face and as usual, he matched from head to toe. Though Roland resembled a younger Clifton Powell, he dressed like Carlton from 'The Fresh Prince'.

"Roland, I'm going to ask you one more time before I have the bitch that replaced you come outside and escorted you to your car. And believe me not all dogs are your best friend. Now, what are you doing at my home? I haven't seen you in over a year. Let's not count the night you popped up."

"Yeah, and I've been calling you ever since then too."

"I don't know why. You made it perfectly clear when you left me to go back to your real life. Your words, not mine."

Taking a step forward, a man that was now a stranger to me, reached for my touch. Sheepishly, he flinched when Connor's voice blared through the intercom.

"Excuse you. The lady asked for some breathing room and my daddy wouldn't be cool with you touching his wife."

Wide-eyed and stunned, I laughed openly. I didn't give a damn about Roland's feelings, Connor's intrusion was funny. Roland didn't deserve my sincerity but our discussion wasn't for her ears.

"Connor, if you don't go –"

"Okay. Okay, I'll go, but if you need me, just scream," she advised, letting the speaker breathe.

"Kross, I was a fool to walk away when you needed me most. When I left, I thought I was missing out on the world staying in the house with you but after being out there I've realized it isn't the same without you. I've been thinking about this for months. Even purchased ten thousand dollars' worth of your jewels to prove it," he bragged

Stunned, I took a step back as if there wasn't already enough distance between us on my porch.

"That was you?"

Smiling, Roland thought my question was a revelation that brought reassurance. Instead, it made me feel…violated.

"Yep. I know how you much love *Vibez*, so I figured I'd… invest. I knew if I showed you I'm still the same man that will buy you the world; you'd give me a shot."

"Wow," I muttered. "Who did you give the jewelry to?"

"Why does that matter? I paid you for them. And now, I'm ready to figure out where we go from here. I can make us a reservation at—"

"Roland! Are you hearing yourself? I'm not going on a damn date with you! And it matters because I want them back," I shrieked.

"Why are you getting all bent out of shape? Don't pretend that bum and little brat have you wrapped around their fingers. You've never been the mothering type," he accused, crushing my feelings a little.

"I know you're still upset but I'm willing to fix this. I can give you whatever you want now that you're willing to come out to get it," he boasted as if it were actually a compliment.

"Roland, it's over. As you said, you couldn't deal with my issues. Guess what? They're still here," I said, pointing my heart.

"The difference in me that has you breaking off your pockets and damn near stalking me, is courtesy of space from you and a man you couldn't see on your worst day filling your spot. You can't buy me nigga! If you've noticed my growth, you should've seen this coming."

"Or me pulling up," Hollis blurted, standing directly behind Roland. Lust clouded my concentration, staring at his body covered by a black tank top and black short. The suburban-bred trespasser tried his best not to allow his anxiety to show but it was impossible not to see. The height difference made it hard to take the scene seriously.

"Didn't I tell you the last time we spoke, get the fuck on?"

Finally facing him, Roland put his shoulders back as he spoke.

"Man, I don't want any problems. Kross and I have history. I just needed to see if there was a chance—"

"That you could try your luck without me breaking your fucking neck?" Hollis ejected. Muting Roland's stutters, the giant put his palm in the center of the short man's face.

"I'm going to ask you once more time and that's only because I know my nosey ass kid is watching us right now. Stay the fuck away from my lady. Respect that," Hollis growled, hostility controlling his tenor.

When Roland turned to look at me, Connor shouted her two cents. "You heard him. Respect our family, sir."

Smiling, my eyes filled with joy my body couldn't contain. Even if I never had my own children, I knew Connor and I had established a bond that not even her hating ass mama could break. I already told her we'd stay in contact no matter how the case went next week; even if we had to get a P.O. Box and write one another. May not have been right but Connor needed positive female reinforcement in her life and I'd go around her mama to make sure she had it.

Out my gate and rounding his overpriced Tesla, Roland shook his head but dared not to utter another word.

"And now, what are *you* doing here?"

"Doesn't matter. Looks like I came right in time," he hinted, nuzzling my hips in his hands.

"Oh, you think so?"

"I know," Hollis commented, staring at me.

"What's wrong?"

"I went to see Kelsey a few days ago."

My heart dropped. I knew nothing I wanted to hear was to follow.

"For what? I mean…how'd that go?"

Shaking his head, Hollis draped my arms around his neck.

"It didn't. I didn't get out of the car. I realized I don't need to have some long, drawn-out conversation with her to have closure. She can't help me work through my trust issues, that's on me."

"Wow, guess you don't need to see Dr. Sway."

"I actually already did," he confessed, not an inch of embarrassment casing over his admission.

Like a proud mama, I beamed. "Really?"

"Really. You were right about me having shit bottled up and I can't give you my all if I don't get everything else out the way. I've decided not to fight Ciara on this child support thing. As long as I could have my kid when I want, I don't want any problems. I'm also thinking about trying this thing with my mom again. Holly's been on me about it. All I can do is try."

"Damn, it's only been weeks since you got the notice and days since I saw you. What the hell did Sway do to you?" I tormented, pressing my hand to the back of his forehead.

"She allowed me to speak freely until I could hear my own self. I know where I want to be, Kross. Just gotta have a clear head to get there."

Leading me to my steps, the smile we wore dropped hearing the ruckus behind us. When I turned I saw a woman I'd never seen behind staring between Hollis and I, and some man dressed in all black.

"Are you really coming over here with this shit, Shelby? You want to be with this nigga that bad? I followed you and this is where you come to?" the man yelled, stalking towards my yard with venom pouring from his mouth. Though I was familiar with the situation, I didn't know it was still a *situation*.

"I wasn't doing anything, Henry. You have no right to follow me."

Chuckling menacingly, Hollis barked. "And you think you do? What the fuck are you doing at my lady's house? I've told you too many times, it's a wrap!" Growing more furious, Henry faced Hollis.

"I trusted you muthafucka'," the scorned man snapped, pulling a gun from his black trench coat and training it on Hollis. My heart skipped a beat.

"What the hell is that supposed to mean?" Hollis questioned. I hated how unfazed he appeared while a gun was aimed at the center of his chest. If his nonchalant demeanor pissed me off, I could only imagine how it made Henry feel.

"I respected you as a man and my boss and you go behind my back and fuck my wife."

Running a hand down his face, Hollis groaned impatiently. "Man, don't get at me with that shit. You're speaking as if I knew she was your wife."

"It doesn't matter, nigga! You knew she belonged to somebody and it wasn't you," Henry spat. The weight of his words hovered over where we stood. "You got this woman by your side and probably playing her like a fucking fiddle."

"Watch yourself. I get that you're hurt but don't put Kross in this. I haven't touch Shelby in over eight months. I've never cheated on my lady, nigga!" Hollis roared, nearing Henry's stance.

Sweat filled Henry's forehead as his nerves revealed themselves despite his warning. "You think I'm playing? I will shoot yo' big ass, homie. Try me!"

Standing so close they could reach out and touch shoulders, both men remained solid in his place. I could see they were serious and didn't plan to bow to the next. Sheepishly, Shelby stood off to the side crying tears that made the tension even heavier.

"Henry! Have you lost your mind? You can't kill this man," she blabbed.

Turning the chrome in her direction, Henry groaned. "You crying over this fool? Sitting outside this broad's house because he's here. You two muthafuckas deserve to be in hell together."

My body shivered seeing the hurt in Henry's eyes blend with anger. I couldn't stand around again and allow someone to put me in the middle of brutality. I knew I'd never make it out of solitude if Hollis was taken from me. He was my solitude and me assuming Connor was inside watching the entire thing, prompted my feet to move.

"Henry, listen to me," I began to say.

"Kross—" Hollis grumbled, latching his hand around my elbow. Deliberately, I pulled away and stepped forward.

"They aren't worth your life. Your freedom."

Like a protective beast, he snarled. "She is. Shelby is worth it."

"But if you take her from the earth then what? You go to jail.

Nobody will care that she tarnished her vows, Henry. Trust me, their selfish actions aren't yours to mimic. If you take something you shouldn't, you're acting like God and as a man adorning a cross around his neck, I have a feeling you know better," I preached, hoping my mention of our Father would hit home.

"Aye," I heard the deep voice that calmed my spirit call from behind me.

When our eyes locked, I mouthed the words "shut up" with tight teeth and round lips. Even in dire situations, he had to be the one doing most of the talking.

Reclaiming my attention, Henry's disposition altered. "This was supposed to be for better or worse. I've always done right by her and this is how she repays me. How are we supposed to get past this and she's still chasing another man?"

Exhaling, I agreed. "As hard as it may be, you have to understand that for some people your all isn't good enough and, that's in no way a reflection of you. That's her fucking problem. People will only remember that you killed her for making a mistake. How fair would that be?"

Slowly Henry's raised hand fell. My feet loosened from the imaginary concrete holding me in place.

"Baby, I'm so sorry. I'm so sorry. I messed up but I love you," Shelby claimed, dropping to her knees like a wounded soldier.

Quietly, Hollis came to my side. Engulfing my hands as if they were his lifeline, he squeezed my fingers. Neither of us thought to disturb the scorned couple's reconciliation, we just accepted the responsibility for being a product of someone else's pain and allowed distance to heal.

"I swear to God, I haven't slept with that woman or anyone else since we've been together. When I told you I was serious about us, I meant it," Hollis stated low enough for only me to hear.

Staring over at him, my face held a half-smile.

"I believe you, Hollis."

"Do you?"

I nodded in response.

"Henry, let's just go home," I heard Shelby propose to the broken man. Lazily, Henry's grasp on the 380 slackened. My eyes stalked the pistol as it sank in slow motion to the pavement and sounded off on impact of crashing with the concrete.

Pow!

A single shot rang out in my front yard banishing time.

None of us moved or made a noise.

Seconds passed before the grumble of Hollis Brown snatched me from my déjà vu. My eyes lowered to where he'd cautiously laid his body down.

"Fuck," he spat in a harsh whisper. Though scared to move and face the damage, hearing Connor's cry rearranged my shock.

"Daddy! Daddy! I'm going to call 911," she yelled, stopping her speed walking and running back into the house to grab the phone.

"It was an accident," Henry shouted repeatedly.

Still unable to completely gauge the situation, I kneeled beside Hollis quietly.

This cannot be happening, my conscious yelled.

"Baby look at me," I wailed, wrapping his hand in mine. The blood spreading across his black shirt was evidence of the chest wound Hollis sustained.

"Just when I was ready to give you the world," he slurred, his demeanor calm and eyes shut.

Through my tears, I smiled. "Stop trying to make me feel good. You're hurt. You're losing a lot of blood, Hollis."

"That's alright. You can just give me some of yours," he declared, his decreased tenor almost too low to make out.

"Let's go, Henry. Let's just go! It was an accident," Shelby mentioned for the second time. I didn't give a damn if it were an accident or not, if Hollis didn't make it there would be hell to pay.

"The ambulance is on their way. Just be strong daddy," Connor encouraged, joining me at her father's side. Seeing the pain, worry, and fear in her eyes caused me to halt even more than seeing Hollis laid out. She was only eight years old and would forever remember this day.

"Daddy, please open your eyes. You're scaring me."

With a deep breath, that appeared to hurt, Hollis did as his baby requested.

"I'm okay, Connor. Please stop crying, baby" he begged, a tear sliding down his face when his eyes found the sky.

Checking our surroundings, I spotted the two cowards rushing away from the scene. By this time my neighbors were on their porches; some recording and others on the phone calling in the crime.

"You're going to be alright, Hollis. You just have to stay awake," I drilled noticing how hard it was for him to do as I asked.

"I love you, Hollis. Don't do this to me. Us. Connor needs you." Caressing his fresh twist, I inhaled the pineapple scent pouring from him.

"As long as you're here, I know she's good and I'll love you forever for that," he mumbled, slipping away from me that quickly.

EPILOGUE
Kross

Life was different, but no one said different wasn't a good thing. I'd gone from hiding to being found and captured by a man who cared nothing about my flaws and was grateful for my best. There weren't enough days in our lifetime for me to repay him for forcing me to go after all the world had to offer; but him allowing me to be a force in his daughter's life was the least I could do to display my gratitude.

Smiling subtly, Dr. Sway exhaled gently.

"What's up with the impromptu session?"

Clearing my throat, I rolled my eyes at the topic that wouldn't seem to fade.

"Well, my husband believes we should have an in-home birth and I don't agree. Considering I'm the one—"

"Here we go with this shit again," Hollis interrupted.

"Excuse you," I shrieked, looking at the man who set beside me like he had two heads.

"See, and this is what I deal with at home. Attitude!"

Waving me off, Hollis leaned forward like his point would reach our mediator quicker.

"Kross, thinks because she's carrying our son, she's the only one who should have a say in how he comes into the world. That's bull—bogus," Hollis declared. Ever since Hollis was shot, he'd become obsessed with holistic medicine and healing. He was completely against me delivering at the hospital, no matter how petrified I was to give birth at home.

Grinning, the observant doctor stared between my husband and I. I knew she was thinking exactly what I had plenty of mornings. Many times, Hollis caught me watching him while he tried to sleep or caught me praying over Connor when she wasn't paying attention.

"Look, Dr. I wasn't present when my daughter was born. I didn't have the opportunity to voice what I felt was best for my kid."

"And what about what's best for mommy?" She questioned. In my head, we shared a high-five.

"Here y'all go with that gang- gang shit."

Snickering, Dr. Sway removed glasses she didn't actually need. "Mr. Brown, we are not ganging up on you. I just want you to recognize Kross has to be healthy, comfortable and stress-free to have the best labor. I do think there are some things you two can incorporate in the next three months that may serve as a compromise?"

"I'm listening."

Elbowing him, I snarled. "Stop being an asshole, Hollis. You asked to stop by."

"Maybe Kross can revisit the topic of breastfeeding, even if just for a little while. You guys can simply look into water baths. Getting some information on the process can't hurt anything."

I smacked my teeth at the latter.

"Kross, have you even considered the notion of having the baby at home."

Jumping in, the anxious man slid his hand into black sweats that matched ones I wore. "Nope, she shut it down because she's afraid. Even when I promised to be by her side she's not even willing to try," he divulged, the disappointment in his tone caused my eyes to water.

Sitting back in his seat, Hollis turned my face in his direction.

"Why are you crying?"

"Because I'm scared but I don't want to disappoint you," I cried softly. Cupping my face, Hollis eyed me intently.

"You are not disappointing me, Kross."

"Yes, I am. I can hear it in your tune."

Interrupting my bubbling tantrum, Dr. Sway cleared her throat.

"Kross, why are you afraid of having your baby naturally."

Swallowing my embarrassment, I was honest with the two folks in the room. I didn't cower under my truth. Other than Truth being a vault for me, Hollis and Sway were just as much of a safe haven.

"I'm afraid I'm not strong enough to bring Kriss into the world without the doctors, medicine and all that. Anything could go wrong and I don't think I could live if my son— yeah."

"And how do you feel about her concerns, Hollis?"

Reaching for my hand, Hollis placed a kiss on the back gently.

"I understand and I respect them. Kross has been my side through the shaky relationship with my mom and my daughter's mom. Even when ole' boy was sentenced to assault for shooting me, she was my backbone. I guess, I just took her protest personal. Like, I couldn't give her the strength she's given me to push our son out naturally. I didn't take what she just said into consideration."

"Kross, had you told Hollis about your concerns."

Sheepishly, I shook my head.

"Come on. You two know better. I thought communication was becoming your strong point after what you've had to worked through in the last year," our therapist playfully teased.

Hollis and I had been coming to see Dr. Sway as a couple, aside from separately for nearly a year. Him almost being gunned down served as a major trigger for me. It took months of distant love and a few after court slip ups to pull me out of my depression and back into the arms I felt safest in. Between Ciara giving up custody of Connor because she thought in some warped way it would hurt Hollis, to him taking a bullet; the strong man himself needed distance then affection. Us getting married was abrupt but necessary. Hollis was my soulmate. No matter how long we stayed apart our souls searched for one another and time nor circumstances could negate that.

"I have an exercise for you guys," Dr. Sway explained when the alarm sounded.

Hollis exhaled openly. "Aww shit."

"I want you two to find one thing you guys don't agree on and compromise on the resolution. It doesn't have to be regarding baby Kriss, just something of significance."

"Tuh, we can start with her going to see her Pimp Daddy. Literally," Hollis clowned. I hadn't spoken to my father since I invited him to my speaking engagement. Though I hadn't made it myself, he had no intention on supporting me. When he realized I was serious about my business plans, he called himself cutting me off. Recently, Kennedy and I found out he was dying from cancer and wanted to see us. Hollis wasn't feeling it. He knew the relationship with my daddy was strained but important to me. Seeing him would cause more stress than I needed to deal with since I'd recently started hosting pop up shops for *Vibez* and that was turning into a bigger project than I'd anticipated though I loved it.

Laughing, Dr. Sway raised a hand.

"I don't want to know what the problem or solution is. Not today anyway. Talk through it with respect and find a common ground," she suggested, opening the door for us to exit.

"Lord, it took you guys long enough. I know my brother is in there starving," Connor complained, jumping from the waiting room seat when she spotted us.

"It was less than thirty minutes and don't start blaming shit on your brother already. He isn't even here yet," Hollis declared, pulling gently on one of Connor's flowing French braids.

"I'm not putting anything on him. I'm looking out like a big sister should. You two have each other, I need my own person," she stated. Walking into the elevator, I frowned at her accusation.

"Connor, you have us too you know. There is no me and daddy. It's the three of us or nothing. You hear me?"

"Yes, Kross. I know you love me and we're a family. You tell me every day! Now, let's go eat!"

Once we entered the parking garage, Hollis pulled me a foot away while Connor got in the car.

"Thank you for that."

Grinning, I rubbed the beard Hollis and Kennedy thought it was okay to be in competition over growing.

"You don't have to thank me baby. I told you when you proposed, Connor was my baby from that day forward. Honestly, our bond was solidified well before the paperwork."

"I know," he proclaimed, circling my expanding waist and rubbing my back so tenderly I could've fallen asleep while standing.

"I know you're aware but you deserve to hear how much I appreciate you. How much I love you for trusting me with your heart and giving me the chance to show you I'd give my life to make sure you're safe. I swear to the heavens, I'm not going anywhere. Wherever you are, that's where I'll be. Forever."

Blushing, I nodded in agreement. "Forever sounds like my type of place."

Afterword

What can I truly say besides thank you! I hope you enjoyed Hollis and Kross' love story as much as I loved writing it. Though there are tender subject matters weaved between their romance, I hope you received the message that second chances are worthy of the faith they require.

To my Soul Sistah, Britt Joni and my pen sis, Lateea (Wynta Tyme), thank you for lending your time and eyes as I constructed this rollercoaster.

I'd like to give a special thanks to my publisher, Ms. B. Love. Your ability to teach and write love is phenomenal. Thank you for trusting me to penning romance, flaws and all!

Let's stay connected

FACEBOOK: Author Tucora Monique
INSTAGRAM: @AuthorTucoraMonique
Twitter: AuthorTucora

Until next time…

TUCORA MONIQUE
FLAWED

B. Love Publications

Visit bit.ly/readBLP to join our mailing list!

B. Love Publications - where Authors celebrate black men, black women, and black love.
To submit a manuscript for consideration, email your first three chapters to blovepublications@gmail.com with SUBMISSION as the subject.

Let's connect on social media!
Facebook - B. Love Publications
Twitter - @blovepub
Instagram - @blovepublications